Tales From Central America

Traditional tales, fables and sagas

from Central America and its peoples.

Compiled, Adapted & Edited by Clive Gilson

Tales from the World's Firesides

Tales From Central America, edited by Clive Gilson,

Solitude, Bath, UK

www.clivegilson.com

First print edition © 2025, Clive Gilson

Printed by IngramSpark

ISBN: 978-1-915081-37-7

- I have edited Clive Gilson's books for over a decade now – he's prolific and can turn his hand to many genres. poetry, short fiction, contemporary novels, folklore, and science fiction – and the common theme is that none of them ever fails to take my breath away. There's something in each story that is either memorably poignant, hauntingly unnerving, or sidesplittingly funny - *Lorna Howarth, The Write Factor*

-

- *Ragged A**** Ruffian reviewed on Amazon in the United Kingdom on 27 January 2021* - A truly heartwarming, interesting, story with a wonderful narrative. Unquestionably a splendid read

- A Solitude of Stars: With deft turns of phrase and an imagination that would make Philip K. Dick jealous, Gilson foresees a dystopian future, the seeds of which are definitely being sown right now. The story is a chilling glimpse of what may come to pass, warmed by a thread of love that raises the narrative beyond despair. I found the stories disturbing and breath-taking in equal measure. The Apparat and Dirigiste tribes are ranging across our solar system seeking peace by waging war, raising the question; is humanity actually capable of peace? A riveting read. - *Rob Swan, The Write Factor*

- Songs of Bliss gripped me from the start - I had to read right to the end. Loved the humour. Impressed by the surprising empathy that I felt for rather - on the face of it - unlikeable characters. Look forward to seeing it in print. - *Maighdean-Mhara, commenting on Authonomy*

- I just wanted to thank you once more for your help acquiring this beautiful collection. It's found a new home at the top of my library. I've already stumbled onto some wonderful stories in a couple of the collections, and I can't wait to get more. Have a wonderful holiday and a great new year... - *Richer Daniel Laporte, California, December 2021*

Interior image: OpenClipart-Vectors from Pixabay

Cover image: by Nishshanka Ruwan from Pixabay

CONTENTS

Preface

I've been collecting and telling stories for a couple of decades now, having had several of my own fictional works published in recent years. My particular focus is on short story writing in the realms of magical realities and science fiction fantasies.

I've always drawn heavily on traditional folk and fairy tales, and in so doing have amassed a digital collection of many thousands of these tales from around the world. It has been one of my long-standing ambitions to gather these stories together and to create a library of tales that tell the stories of places and peoples from all corners of our world.

One of the main motivations for me in undertaking the project is to collect and tell stories that otherwise might be lost or, at best, be forgotten by predominantly English-speaking readers. Given that a lot of my sources are from early collectors, particularly covering works produced in the late eighteenth century, throughout the nineteenth century, and in the early years of the twentieth century, I do make every effort to adapt stories for a modern reader. Early collectors had a different world view to many of us today, and often expressed views about race and gender, for example, that we find difficult to reconcile in the early years of the twenty-first century. I try, although with varying degrees of success, to update these stories with sensitivity while trying to stay as true to the original spirit of each story as I can.

I also want to assure readers that I try hard not to comment on or appropriate originating cultures. It is almost certainly true that the early collectors of these tales, with their then prevalent world views, have made assumptions about the originating cultures that have given us these tales. I hope that you'll accept my mission to preserve these tales, however and wherever I find them, as just that. I have, therefore, made sure that every story has a full attribution, covering both the original collector / writer and the collection title that this version has been adapted from, as well as having notes about publishers and other relevant and, I hope, interesting source data. Wherever possible I have added a cultural or indigenous attribution as well, although for some of the titles, the country-based theme is obvious.

This volume, *Tales From Central America,* is the first in what I hope will be a small set of collections covering tales from Central and South America, an area that actually covers a whole host of nations and storytelling traditions.

These folk tales, legends, and fairy tales are rich with cultural heritage and often reflect the unique blend of indigenous, European, and other cultural influences found in the region.

Many Central American folk tales and legends incorporate elements from indigenous cultures such as the Aztec, Maya, Zapotec, and others. These stories often feature mythological beings, gods, and spirits from pre-Columbian belief systems.

Central American folklore often exhibits syncretism, the merging of different cultural or religious beliefs. This is evident in the blending of indigenous myths and rituals with Catholicism, which was introduced by the Spanish during colonization.

Central American folk tales frequently contain elements of magical realism, where fantastical events are portrayed in a matter-of-fact manner, blurring the lines between the ordinary and the supernatural.

Central America's diverse geography and cultural heritage have given rise to a wide range of regional folk tales and legends. Each region has its own unique stories, characters, and themes, reflecting local traditions, landscapes, and historical events.

Many of these folk tales and legends explore themes of resilience, survival, and identity, often reflecting the struggles and triumphs of the Mexican people throughout history.

Central American folklore features a variety of iconic characters such as La Llorona (the Weeping Woman), El Chupacabra (the Goat Sucker), and many others, each with their own symbolic significance and cultural resonance.

Overall, Central American folk tales, legends, and fairy tales offer a fascinating glimpse into the cultural tapestry of the region, highlighting its rich history, traditions, and worldview.

These collections will grow over coming years to tell lost and forgotten tales from every continent, and even then, I'll just be scratching the surface of the world's lore and love. That's the great gift in storytelling. Since the first of our ancestors sat around in a cave, contemplating an ape's place in the world, we have, as a species, continued to tell each other stories of magic and cunning and caution and love. All those years ago, when I began to read through tales from the Celts, tales from Indonesia, tales from Africa and the Far East, tales from everywhere, one of the things that struck me clearly was just how similar are our roots. We share characters and characteristics. The nature of these tales is so similar underneath the local camouflage. Human beings clearly share a storytelling heritage so much deeper than the world that we see superficially as always having been just as it is now.

These tales were originally told by firelight as a way of preserving histories and educating both adult and child. These tales form part of our shared heritage, witches, warts, fantastic beasts, and all. They can be dark and violent. They can be sweet and loving. They are we and we are they in so many ways. I've loved reading and re-reading these stories. I hope that you do too.

Clive

Bath 2025

Quetzalcoatl

This story has been adapted from a tale originally told by Lewis Spence in The Myths Of Mexico & Peru, published in 1913 by Thomas Y. Crowell Company, New York. The Myths of Mexico & Peru provides an overview of the rich mythological traditions of these ancient civilizations, drawing upon archaeological evidence, historical accounts, and indigenous sources. Spence's work delves into various aspects of Mesoamerican and Andean cosmology, religion, rituals, deities, and legendary figures, offering insights into the cultural and spiritual beliefs of these societies.

Quetzalcoatl was known as "The Father of the Toltecs," and according to legend, he was the youngest of seven sons born to Iztacmixcohuatl, the Toltec equivalent of Abraham. His name, which means "Feathered Serpent" or "Feathered Staff," became synonymous with wisdom and leadership. At an early age, he rose to power as the ruler of Tollan, where his enlightened rule and support for the arts helped advance Toltec civilization.

His reign was long enough to establish a strong foundation for Toltec culture, but trouble arrived in the form of two powerful sorcerers: Tezcatlipoca and Coyotlinaual, god of the Amantecas.

Tezcatlipoca, descending from the sky on a fine web like a spider, tricked Quetzalcoatl into drinking pulque, a fermented drink. Intoxicated, Quetzalcoatl lost his self-control and broke his vow of chastity with Quetzalpetlatl. As a result, he was banished from Anahuac. His departure brought dramatic changes to the land. He hid his treasures of gold and silver, burned his palaces, transformed cacao trees into mezquites, and drove birds away from Tollan. The sorcerers, taken aback by these events, pleaded for his return, but he refused, saying the sun needed him elsewhere.

Quetzalcoatl journeyed to Tabasco and Tlapallan, the legendary land of the east. He threw himself onto a funeral pyre, and as his body burned, his ashes rose into the sky, transforming into brilliantly coloured birds. His heart ascended into the heavens and became the morning star.

The Mexicans believed that Quetzalcoatl's death coincided with the first appearance of the morning star, earning him the title "Lord of the Dawn." According to their traditions, he was invisible for four days after his death and then wandered the underworld for eight more days. When the morning star finally shone, it signified his resurrection and his ascension as a god.

Myths of Quetzalcoatl and Tezcatlipoca

This story has also been adapted from a tale originally told by Lewis Spence in The Myths Of Mexico & Peru, published in 1913 by Thomas Y. Crowell Company, New York.

During the time of Quetzalcoatl, the people lived in abundance. Corn was plentiful, gourds grew as thick as a man's arm, and cotton sprouted in every colour without needing to be dyed. The air was alive with the songs of brilliantly coloured birds, and gold, silver, and precious gems were everywhere. Under Quetzalcoatl's rule, peace and prosperity flourished for all.

But such happiness could not last. Envious of Quetzalcoatl and the prosperity of the Toltecs, three malevolent sorcerers conspired against them. These sorcerers were, in reality, gods of the invading Nahua tribes, Huitzilopochtli, Titlacahuan (Tezcatlipoca), and Tlacahuepan. Determined to bring down Tollan, they cast dark spells over the city, with Tezcatlipoca leading the deception.

Disguised as an old man with white hair, Tezcatlipoca arrived at Quetzalcoatl's palace and addressed the attendants:

"Please take me to your master. I have something important to discuss with him."

The attendants hesitated, explaining that Quetzalcoatl was unwell and unable to receive visitors. But the old man insisted, urging them to announce his arrival. Reluctantly, they did so, and Quetzalcoatl agreed to let him in.

Inside, Tezcatlipoca feigned sympathy for the suffering god-king.

"How are you, my son?" he asked. "I have brought you a special drink that will cure your illness."

Quetzalcoatl welcomed him, saying, "I knew you would come. My sickness has worsened, I can barely move my hands or feet."

Tezcatlipoca reassured him, promising that the potion he carried would restore his health. Desperate for relief, Quetzalcoatl drank it and immediately felt stronger. Seeing this, Tezcatlipoca urged him to drink more, offering cup after cup.

But the so-called medicine was pulque, the fermented wine of the land. As Quetzalcoatl drank, he became intoxicated, losing control of himself. Now drunk and vulnerable, he was at the mercy of his enemy, a god tricked by a god, his fate sealed in deception.

Tezcatlipoca and the Toltecs

This story has been adapted from a tale originally told by Lewis Spence in The Myths Of Mexico & Peru, published in 1913 by Thomas Y. Crowell Company, New York. The Myths of Mexico & Peru provides an overview of the rich mythological traditions of these ancient civilizations, drawing upon archaeological evidence, historical accounts, and indigenous sources. Spence's work delves into various aspects of Mesoamerican and Andean cosmology, religion, rituals, deities, and legendary figures, offering insights into the cultural and spiritual beliefs of these societies.

Tezcatlipoca, determined to bring about the downfall of the Toltec state, disguised himself as an ordinary man named Toueyo (or Toveyo) and made his way to the palace of Uemac, the ruler of the Toltecs in worldly affairs. Uemac had a daughter renowned for her beauty, and though many suitors sought her hand in marriage, her father refused them all.

One day, as she looked out from the palace, she saw the disguised Tezcatlipoca walking past and was instantly overcome with love for him. Her desire for him grew so intense that she fell gravely ill. When Uemac learned of his daughter's sickness, he visited her chambers and asked her attendants what had caused her suffering. They revealed that she had fallen deeply in love with a mysterious Indian traveller who had recently passed by.

Determined to remedy the situation, Uemac ordered Toueyo's arrest, and the stranger was brought before him. "Where do you come from?" Uemac demanded, noting the man's unusual and scant clothing.

"My lord, I am a traveller, and I have come here to sell green paint," replied Tezcatlipoca.

"Why are you dressed this way? Where is your cloak?" Uemac questioned.

"My lord, this is the custom of my homeland," Tezcatlipoca answered.

Uemac then addressed him sternly. "You have stirred forbidden passion in my daughter's heart. What should be done with you for bringing shame upon my house?"

Tezcatlipoca, feigning indifference, simply replied, "Kill me if you must, I do not care."

But Uemac hesitated. "If I take your life, my daughter may not survive," he reasoned. "Instead, you shall marry her."

The marriage between Toueyo and Uemac's daughter caused great unrest among the Toltecs, who murmured among themselves, questioning why their ruler had given his daughter to a mere stranger. Uemac, sensing the growing dissatisfaction, sought to distract his people by declaring war on the neighboring state of Coatepec.

As the Toltec warriors prepared for battle, they devised a plan to rid themselves of Toueyo, placing him and his small band of followers in an exposed position, hoping the enemy would kill him. But instead of being slain, Toueyo and his men triumphed, slaying a great number of Coatepec's warriors and putting the rest to flight.

To celebrate his unexpected victory, Uemac honoured him with elaborate ceremonies, crowning him with knightly plumes and painting his body red and yellow, distinctions reserved for the bravest warriors.

Tezcatlipoca's next move was to invite all the people of Tollan to a grand festival. Massive crowds gathered, dancing and singing to the rhythm of his drum. As Tezcatlipoca led the song, he urged them to keep up with the beat, pushing them to dance faster and faster. The people became frenzied, their movements growing uncontrollable, until they lost all sense of reason. Many, unable to stop, tumbled down a steep ravine and were transformed into rocks. Others, attempting to cross a stone bridge in their madness, fell into the water below, where they too turned to stone.

On another occasion, Tezcatlipoca took on the guise of a warrior named Tequiua and invited the people of Tollan to gather in the beautiful flower garden of Xochitla. When the crowd had assembled, he suddenly attacked them with a hoe, slaughtering many. In their panic, others trampled their fellow Toltecs to death in their desperate attempt to escape.

Yet another time, Tezcatlipoca and Tlacahuepan appeared in the marketplace of Tollan, where Tezcatlipoca held a tiny infant in his palm, making it dance and perform mesmerizing tricks. This child was none other than Huitzilopochtli, the Nahua god of war. Eager to witness this strange spectacle, the Toltecs pressed forward, crushing one another in their excitement, resulting in the deaths of many. Furious at the chaos, the Toltecs, following the advice of Tlacahuepan, captured and executed both Tezcatlipoca and Huitzilopochtli.

But their vengeance brought disaster upon them. The bodies of the fallen gods emitted a terrible stench, spreading a deadly plague that wiped out thousands of Toltecs. Once again, Tlacahuepan urged them to cast the corpses out of the city before the devastation worsened. However, when the Toltecs attempted to move the bodies, they found them impossibly heavy. Hundreds of men wrapped cords around them, only to have the ropes snap under the immense weight. Those who pulled at the cords collapsed and died on the spot, suffocating under the mass of fallen bodies.

Thus, through deception, war, madness, and pestilence, Tezcatlipoca orchestrated the downfall of Tollan, bringing ruin to the once-great Toltec civilization.

The Departure of Quetzalcoatl

This story has also been adapted from a tale originally told by Lewis Spence in The Myths Of Mexico & Peru, published in 1913 by Thomas Y. Crowell Company, New York.

The Toltecs suffered greatly under the enchantments of Tezcatlipoca, and it soon became clear that their empire was in decline. Realizing that the end was near, Quetzalcoatl, disheartened by these events, decided to leave Tollan and return to Tlapallan, the land from which he had originally come to bring civilization to Mexico. Before departing, he burned the houses he had built and buried his treasures of gold and precious stones deep in the valleys between the mountains. He transformed the cacao trees into mezquites and commanded all the brightly coloured and melodious birds to leave the valley of Anahuac and follow him for more than a hundred leagues.

As he journeyed from Tollan, he came across a great tree in a place called Quauhtitlan. There, he rested and asked his attendants for a mirror. Gazing at his reflection in its polished surface, he sighed, "I am old." From this moment, the place became known as Huehuequauhtitlan, or "Old Quauhtitlan." Continuing his journey, he was accompanied by musicians playing flutes. Eventually, exhaustion overcame him, and he sat upon a stone, leaving the imprint of his hands on its surface. This place became known as Temacpalco, "The Impress of the Hands."

At Coaapan, he encountered the Nahua gods, who were hostile toward him and the Toltecs. They confronted him, asking, "Where are you going? Why do you abandon your city?"

"I am going to Tlapallan," Quetzalcoatl replied, "the land from which I came."

"And why do you go?" the enchanters pressed.

"My father, the Sun, has called me back," he answered.

"Then go in peace," they said, "but before you leave, share with us the knowledge of your arts, the secret of working silver, crafting precious stones and fine woods, painting, feather-working, and other skills."

Quetzalcoatl refused and instead cast all his treasures into the waters of Cozcaapa, the "Water of Precious Stones."

At Cochtan, he encountered another enchanter who asked where he was headed. When Quetzalcoatl told him of his destination, the enchanter offered him a drink of wine. After tasting it, Quetzalcoatl fell into a deep sleep.

When he awoke the next morning, he continued his journey. Passing between a volcano and the Sierra Nevada, the cold proved fatal for all his attendants, who perished from exposure. Deeply mourning their loss, Quetzalcoatl wept and sang sorrowful songs for them.

Upon reaching the peak of Mount Poyauhtecatl, he descended swiftly to its base. Finally, he arrived at the sea, where he stepped onto a raft of serpents and was carried away toward Tlapallan.

Huitzilopochtli, the War-God

As with other stories in this opening section, this story has been adapted from a tale originally told by Lewis Spence in The Myths Of Mexico & Peru, published in 1913 by Thomas Y. Crowell Company, New York.

Beneath the towering mountain of Coatepec, near the great Toltec city of Tollan, lived a devout widow named Coatlicue. She was the mother of the Centzonuitznaua, a tribe of warriors, and had a daughter named Coyolxauhqui. Every day, Coatlicue climbed a small hill to pray to the gods in humility and devotion.

One day, as she was deep in prayer, a small ball of vibrant feathers drifted down from the sky and landed upon her. Struck by its beauty, she placed it against her chest, intending to offer it as a gift to the sun god. But soon after, she realized she was pregnant.

When her sons learned of this, they were outraged. They mocked and shamed their mother, convinced that her pregnancy dishonoured them. Coyolxauhqui, their sister, fuelled their anger and urged them to take revenge.

Filled with fear and sorrow, Coatlicue suffered under their scorn. But within her, the voice of her unborn child spoke to her, offering comfort and strength. Meanwhile, her sons plotted against her, vowing to kill her and erase the disgrace they believed she had brought upon their family. Donning their battle gear, they prepared for war, their hair tied in the fashion of warriors.

Among them, however, one brother, Quauitlicac, hesitated. Overcome with doubt, he sought out the unborn child, Huitzilopochtli, and revealed his brothers' plan.

"O brother," said the yet-to-be-born god, "I already know what is coming."

Determined to carry out their plan, the warriors, led by Coyolxauhqui, marched toward Coatlicue, fully armed and carrying bundles of deadly darts.

As they advanced, Quauitlicac hurried to the mountain to warn Huitzilopochtli of their approach.

"Where are they now?" asked Huitzilopochtli.

"They have reached Tzompantitlan," Quauitlicac replied.

A little later, Huitzilopochtli asked again, "And now?"

"They are at Coaxalco," came the response.

Again, Huitzilopochtli inquired, "How far have they come?"

"They are at Petlac," said Quauitlicac.

Finally, Quauitlicac rushed to tell him, "The Centzonuitznaua are here. Coyolxauhqui leads them."

At that very moment, Huitzilopochtli was born, fully armed with a blue shield and spear, his body painted in divine colours. His head was adorned with a grand feathered headdress, and his left leg shimmered with plumes.

With a flash of lightning shaped like a serpent, he struck down Coyolxauhqui, shattering her where she stood. Then, with overwhelming force, he chased after the Centzonuitznaua, pursuing them four times around the mountain.

The warriors, terrified, did not stand and fight. Instead, they fled in panic. Many ran toward the lake, where they drowned in despair. Only a few survived, retreating to Uitzlampa, where they surrendered to Huitzilopochtli and laid down their weapons.

Thus, Huitzilopochtli, the warrior god, was born in battle, proving his strength and securing his place as the supreme protector of his people.

The Lizard and the Sun

This story is my own adaptation of a traditional regional tale. This version of the tale was largely informed by sources from Mexico.

Long ago, in the heart of ancient Mexico, beneath the vast sky where the sun burned golden and fierce, there lived a small but remarkably clever lizard named Tepoztecatl. He was not the strongest nor the fastest among the desert's creatures, but he was certainly the wisest. His quick mind and boundless resourcefulness had earned him a reputation across the sun-scorched land, where even the coyotes and eagles spoke of his cunning.

Yet, despite all his intelligence, Tepoztecatl faced a great challenge, one that even his wit could not easily solve. The desert heat was growing unbearable, more relentless than ever before. Each day, as he lay basking on his favourite rock, the scorching rays burned hotter and hotter, leaving him weak and weary. His scales, usually smooth and cool, felt like embers in a fire. The sand, once a comfortable bed, now seared his tiny feet with every step.

"This cannot go on," Tepoztecatl muttered to himself, his tiny chest rising and falling with laboured breaths. "If I do nothing, I will be baked like a poor grasshopper on a stone!"

Determined to find a solution, Tepoztecatl set off across the desert, weaving between towering cacti, rocky cliffs, and dried riverbeds. He sought out the wisest creatures, hoping one of them might hold the secret to escaping the Sun's unrelenting gaze.

He first came upon an ancient cactus, its arms raised toward the sky like a sage deep in thought. "Oh great cactus," Tepoztecatl pleaded, "you have stood here for centuries, enduring the Sun's fury. Tell me, how do you survive this heat?"

The cactus sighed, with a soft rustling in the wind. "Patience and endurance, little one," it said. "I store the water from the rains and wait for the coolness of night."

Tepoztecatl frowned. "I cannot store water within me. I need relief now, not when the night comes." With a bow of thanks, he pressed on, his feet kicking up golden dust as he made his way through the dunes.

He next sought out Owl, the keeper of wisdom, who sat perched in the hollow of a great tree, blinking slowly in the midday glare.

"Wise Owl," Tepoztecatl called, "you see all, you know all. Surely you have an answer to my plight!"

The Owl blinked twice before speaking. "The Sun is mighty, and none can change its course," she hooted. "If you wish to escape its heat, you must learn to walk only in the shadows."

Tepoztecatl sighed. "But what if the shadows are too far away? What if there is no place to hide?"

The Owl simply shrugged her feathered wings and returned to her slumber.

Frustrated but undaunted, Tepoztecatl continued his quest. At last, after many days of wandering, he came upon Coyote, the trickster of the desert, whose eyes gleamed with mischief and knowing.

"Oh clever Coyote," Tepoztecatl called, "surely you have outwitted the Sun before! Tell me how I may do the same!"

Coyote laughed, a sound like whispering wind through dry grass. "Oh, little lizard, even I do not dare to trick the Sun. But if you wish to change your fate, you must seek out the Sun itself and demand an answer!"

Tepoztecatl's heart pounded at the idea. Speak to the Sun? Face the great burning god of the sky? It seemed impossible, and yet, what other choice did he have? With newfound resolve, he clawed his way up the highest peak, the mountain where only the eagles dared to fly, and at its summit, he called out to the Sun.

The Sun, magnificent and golden, paused in its eternal journey across the sky to regard the tiny lizard standing below. "Who dares summon me?" it rumbled, its voice like the crackling of a great fire.

Tepoztecatl bowed deeply. "Oh mighty Sun, I am but a humble lizard. But your heat has become unbearable, and I beg you for relief!"

The Sun regarded him for a moment, then said, "I cannot dim my rays for one creature alone. My light gives life to the world."

But Tepoztecatl was not so easily discouraged. He thought quickly, then smiled. "If I cannot ask you to dim your light, perhaps I can offer you something instead!"

"Oh?" The Sun's curiosity was piqued. "And what could a tiny creature like you possibly offer me?"

Tepoztecatl grinned. "A dance," he declared, "a dance so dazzling, so mesmerizing, that it will make you forget your own heat!"

The Sun, amused by such boldness, agreed. "Very well, little one. Show me this dance."

And so, Tepoztecatl danced.

He twirled and leapt, his scales shimmering like molten gold. He moved with the grace of a river, the swiftness of the wind, and the joy of the rain. His tiny feet kicked up dust, which swirled around him like a whirlwind of fire and light.

The Sun watched in awe, captivated by the beauty and spirit of the performance. And as it watched, something miraculous happened. The heat lessened, a cool breeze stirred, and for the first time in many days, the desert exhaled in relief.

When Tepoztecatl finally came to a stop, panting but triumphant, the Sun laughed warmly. "You are clever indeed, little lizard. Your dance has brought me joy, and for that, I shall grant you a gift."

The Sun's light shimmered as it spoke. "From this day forward, whenever you seek refuge from my heat, simply rest beneath a rock, or in the shadow of a tree, and there you shall find coolness and comfort."

With gratitude overflowing in his heart, Tepoztecatl bowed low. "Thank you, great Sun. I shall treasure this gift always."

And so, from that day on, whenever the desert sun blazed fiercely, the lizards of the land knew exactly what to do. They found shade, and they rested, forever carrying the legacy of Tepoztecatl's dance within them. And even now, when the desert wind blows and the shadows stretch long, some say that if you listen closely, you can still hear the whispers of the Sun, laughing in delight at the memory of the little lizard who danced among the flames.

19

The Happy Island

This story has been adapted from a tale originally told by Frona Eunice Watt in Tales Of El Dorado, published in 1904 by A.C. McClurg & Co, Chicago. The collection offers a blend of adventure, romance, and intrigue, drawing upon the allure and mystery of the legendary city to weave captivating tales.

A long time ago there was a beautiful island close by the place in the east where the sun rises. The sea was all around it, and at noonday the sun in the sky seemed to slant just above it. Being near the equator and in a tropic clime the winds were soft and warm and full of the odour of sweet flowers. Sometimes the sea was smooth and clear as glass and then the goldfish and sea mosses floated near the surface and glittered in the sunlight.

At night the moon came out big and round like a silver ball and the stars shone very clear because there was no smoke nor fog in the air. In the moonlight the queer little flying fish would jump up out of the water and dart back and forth in the funniest way as if they were playing some kind of game. Their tiny wet wings glistened like silver gauze, and, when everything else was still, made a peculiar whirring sound by all flapping at once.

The beach was strewn with quantities of conch and abalone shells, also other species of all shapes and sizes and they were as dainty in colour as it is possible to imagine. The children of the Happy Island often held the larger ones to their ears to listen to the murmurs and complaints of the insects and other forms of life living inside them. This was only a fancy, but many seashells do have a soft musical cadence if we care to hear it. Some poets believe that they were the first musical instruments, and that the inhabitants of the sea send messages ashore in this manner.

The ferns grew almost as tall as the trees and there were hundreds of birds skimming through the air, or flitting through the branches singing and chattering and having a very happy time. They were not afraid because no one threw stones at them or tried to frighten them. Everybody was glad to see them put up their little bills and ruffle up their throats in singing, or else spread out their wings and splash water all over their backs while they stood on a pebble or twig taking a morning bath. The people said that when the birds were twittering and chirping they were talking to each other. When they were singing they were telling God how thankful they were for the warm sunshine and plenty to eat.

There was a wonderful city in the centre of the island named the City of the Golden Gates because it was surrounded by a high wall of very thick stones, with a great number of gates of gold through which the animals and people passed in and out. Here lived the Old Man of the Sea, as the king was called, and his son was a beautiful youth known as the Golden Hearted because he was so gentle and kind. He was a swift runner and could shoot well with a bow and arrow and was strong enough to wrestle with a big man, but he preferred to make gold ornaments and vessels for his father and was often permitted to go into the king's treasure house to watch the workmen polish the precious gems which they found in great abundance by digging into the mountains near the city.

The people knew all about white and black pearls and how to get them from the bed of the ocean. In full sight of the island was a large reef of pink and white coral and the young prince went there many times to see the curious little insects building their graceful, airy houses over some rock hidden by the water. He sometimes imagined that he heard the mermaids calling to him. What he really did hear was the wind dashing the waves in and out of the coral chambers as if it were determined to wash them away. The reef was an excellent place to fish, and the Golden Hearted and his companions had many a fine day's sport there while the divers were searching for the pearl oysters. He fished with a drag-net made by himself, and he could let it out and haul it in again like a regular sailor. He never killed any of the fish, and the divers would not give him the pearls they found because they were compelled to kill the oysters to get them, and this they said made the pearls unlucky and was the reason why they are round and shining like tear drops. The miners brought him all the emeralds they could find, because this was the happiness-bringing stone. Its colour is like the soft grass in the springtime, and they wanted him to be always young and have everything his heart desired.

The royal gardens were his special care and in them he was allowed to cultivate any kind of tree or plant or grain. Then from them he must learn the names and habits of the trees producing the best wood for building houses, what plants were good to heal the sick, and all about the grains useful for food either for man or animals. Every flower that had a perfume grew in a separate part of the garden, and those shedding their fragrance at night only were in a bed by themselves. He was required to know the difference between single and double species and why there is such a difference in the same family of plants.

Honeybees, big-winged butterflies, crickets and beetles hid in the flowers or flew above them, and these all taught a lesson to the young prince who had no other books. The honeybee was an industrious little fellow continually building a piece of comb or else filling it with honey. The butterfly, on the other hand, did not work at all but changed from an ugly grub into a caterpillar and finally into a gorgeous butterfly with spotted wings and bright eyes. The king told his son that the butterfly was like a soul, the immortal part of us, and he wished him to be as busy as the bee, and to do no more harm to other creatures than does the pretty butterfly.

The cricket was a cheerful, merry chap, usually singing at the top of his voice, and the beetle tried to push all of the dirt out of the garden. If he found anything he did not like he would roll and tumble with it, even if it were much bigger than himself. This amused the Golden Hearted very much, and when he grew tired of his own occupations he would run out into the garden and watch the beetles.

One day he went into the splendid throne-room where his father was giving audience to some wise old men who were foretelling what was going to happen to the king and the people of the Happy Island. They urged the king to send some member of his household to the strange land over the sea, toward the setting sun, where the people were in barbarism.

The Golden Hearted was much interested and thought here was an opportunity to do some good for the weak and helpless. Springing forward he said, "Dear father, let me go. I am able to sail the seas and am willing to devote my life to teaching these poor people how to live like brothers."

The king felt proud of the young prince, but he loved him so dearly that it was hard to let him go, and also hard to refuse such a noble, manly request.

"Do you know, my son, this will entail a great deal of hardship and self-denial?" he asked.

"Yes, father, but God intends us to earn all the good things in life; He will not give them to us for nothing. That is His good law, which makes us healthy, happy and wise, three of the most precious possessions in the world."

"Go, my Golden Heart, and may God bless and keep you always," said the king. "Take a green-throated humming-bird for your guide, and when you find the land, journey on until you come to a place where a cactus grows at the base of a rock and there is a golden eagle soaring in the air above it. Halt there and found a city, and name it in honour of the sun."

Then all the wise men begged to go with him, and for days after there were great preparations made for the departure of the king's son. At daybreak one morning he set sail in a snake-skin boat, and all the inhabitants came with the king to throw flowers and emeralds into the sea because they wished to show respect to the Golden Hearted. It was their method of blessing him and wishing him good luck. The whole shoreline, as far as he could see, was lighted up by bonfires where the people burned resin and perfume to commemorate his going.

At the water's edge stood the old sea king with his long white hair and beard blowing in the wind. By his side was a cream-white horse with three plumes in the top of its bridle reins and a square, red blanket edged with a deep fringe on its back. Crowns and moons and stars of gold and silver were scattered over the blanket to show that the horse belonged to the royal prince. Back of the king was a long line of young warrior priests mounted on white horses, with red blankets, and carrying reversed spears in their hands. They bowed their heads when the poor old father leaned over on the horse's neck and cried as if his heart would break as the boat with his only son in it pushed off from the shore. Snatching a torch from the hand of an attendant, the Golden Hearted waved it on high. Fire with them was a symbol of wisdom, and when the king saw it, he answered the signal by waving a torch, and the warrior priests flashed their spears in the bright sunlight, and the people sent up a deafening shout.

This meant that they were willing to sacrifice their future king for the good of a strange race of men who needed a teacher to show them how to cultivate the land and how to build cities and live civilized. The people of the Happy Island would not send a common man for a teacher. No, indeed, they gave the best they had, their dearly loved prince with the golden heart, to help their less fortunate neighbours. And he gave up all luxury and comfort because he would rather be useful, than live in ease as a king. The name of the island was Atlantis, and the new country was America.

Creation-Story of the Mixtecs

This story has been adapted from a tale originally told by Lewis Spence in The Myths Of Mexico & Peru, published in 1913 by Thomas Y. Crowell Company, New York. The Myths of Mexico & Peru provides an overview of the rich mythological traditions of these ancient civilizations, drawing upon archaeological evidence, historical accounts, and indigenous sources. Spence's work delves into various aspects of Mesoamerican and Andean cosmology, religion, rituals, deities, and legendary figures, offering insights into the cultural and spiritual beliefs of these societies.

In the beginning, when the earth first rose from the primordial waters, two powerful gods appeared: the deer-god, Puma-Snake, and the deer-goddess, Jaguar-Snake. Though they were gods of the deer, they took on human form and, using their immense knowledge and magic, created a towering cliff above the water. Atop this cliff, they built magnificent palaces as their home.

At the summit of the cliff, they placed a copper axe with its sharp edge facing upward, and it was upon this axe that the heavens rested.

This sacred place stood in Upper Mixteca, near Apoala, and became known as the Place Where the Heavens Stood. For centuries, the two gods lived there happily.

After many years, the deer-gods had two sons, Wind-Nine-Snake and Wind-Nine-Cave. From birth, they were remarkably skilled, possessing great wisdom and knowledge of the supernatural arts. They could transform into an eagle or a snake, make themselves invisible, and even pass through solid objects. Their parents devoted great care to their education, ensuring they mastered their divine abilities.

As the young gods grew, they felt the need to honour their ancestors. They prepared ceremonial incense burners made of clay, filled them with tobacco, and set them smouldering. The rising smoke was the first-ever offering to the gods.

Next, they created a garden, planting shrubs, flowers, fruit trees, and fragrant herbs. Beside it, they prepared a grassy clearing, where they placed everything needed for sacred rituals. In this space, the brothers lived peacefully, tending their garden, burning tobacco, and offering prayers.

They pleaded with their ancestors to bring forth the light, gather the waters into rivers and lakes, and reveal the earth hidden beneath the endless sea, for they had nothing but their small garden to live on. To strengthen their prayers, they practiced ritual bloodletting, piercing their ears and tongues with flint knives and sprinkling their blood onto the plants using willow branches.

Over time, the deer-gods had many more children, but disaster struck. The Great Flood came, and many of their descendants perished in the waters. When the flood finally receded, a powerful deity known as the Creator of All Things stepped forward. With divine might, this god reformed the heavens and the earth and restored the human race, allowing life to begin anew.

The Mexican Noah

This story has also been adapted from a tale originally told by Lewis Spence in The Myths Of Mexico & Peru, published in 1913 by Thomas Y. Crowell Company, New York.

In the year of Ce-calli, disaster struck on the very first day. A massive flood submerged the mountain, and the waters remained still for fifty-two years.

As the year neared its end, the god Titlacahuan warned a man named Nata and his wife Nena, saying, "Stop making pulque and listen carefully. Hollow out a large cypress tree immediately. When the month of Tozoztli arrives and the waters rise to the sky, take shelter inside."

Following his instructions, Nata and Nena entered the cypress. Before closing the door, Titlacahuan told them, "You may each eat only one ear of maize."

When the flood finally receded, the cypress stopped floating, and the couple cautiously stepped outside. The world had changed, the land was quiet, and the waters had calmed. Inside the cypress, they found it had filled with fish. Using pieces of wood, they started a fire by rubbing them together and roasted the fish for food.

Watching from the heavens, the gods Citallinicue and Citallatonac noticed the smoke rising and asked, "What is that fire? Why is it reaching the sky?"

Titlacahuan-Tezcatlipoca immediately descended to investigate. Seeing Nata and Nena cooking, he scolded them: "What is the meaning of this fire?" Then, as punishment, he transformed the fish they had been roasting into dogs by reshaping their bodies and changing their heads.

La Patasola

This story is my own adaptation of a traditional regional tale. This version of the tale was largely informed by sources from Colombia.

The Colombian jungle whispers with dread when night falls. Beneath its towering canopy, where the trees weave a web of shadow, something lurks, a creature neither fully woman nor fully beast. It is La Patasola.

Long ago, in a village now swallowed by the green abyss of the jungle, there lived a woman both envied and adored. Her name is long forgotten, but her beauty was spoken of in hushed reverence. Her hair cascaded like black silk, her emerald-green eyes shimmered like cursed jewels, and her laughter, oh, how it sang through the trees, captivating even the birds that dared to listen. But beauty often invites envy, and love, when tainted by betrayal, can become a venom stronger than any poison.

Her husband, a hunter known for his sharp blade and sharper tongue, was not content with his wife alone. He let his lust guide him, seeking the warmth of another. When she discovered his treachery, her heart did not shatter, it burned. Mad with grief and consumed by a rage so potent it tainted the very air, she prayed for vengeance.

No one knows who or what heard her cries, perhaps the jungle itself, perhaps something older and hungrier. That night, as a storm howled through the village, the woman was taken. Some say the earth split open, swallowing her whole. Others whisper that she was dragged away by shadowed hands, her screams swallowed by the wailing wind. By dawn, she was gone. What returned was not the woman they once knew.

From that day onwards, through the fog-drenched jungle, La Patasola hunts, her twisted form moving with an unnatural grace. She is no longer wholly woman. Her one leg, long and sinewy, bends like that of a beast, yet carries her with eerie swiftness. Her hands, once delicate, now end in curved, blackened claws, sharp enough to slice through bone. And her face... when her victims see her true face, it is already too late.

She does not kill quickly.

To the lustful men who fall for her beauty, she grants them one last moment of false hope before their world turns to screams. As their lips near hers, as their fingers brush against her cold skin, her form twists, revealing a monstrous visage of hollowed eyes, jagged fangs, and hunger unending.

They never escape whole.

To the lost children, she sings soft lullabies, drawing them deeper into the jungle, cradling them in arms that feel too strong, too sharp, too wrong. What happens next is known only to the jungle, but their cries are never heard again.

Yet, for all her violence, some say La Patasola still weeps. On certain nights, when the moon hangs too low and the jungle seems to breathe, her wails rise above the trees. They say she mourns what she once was, that somewhere beneath the cursed flesh and hunger, the woman remains, trapped, tormented, and forever vengeful.

But do not pity her.

For if you hear her sobs too closely, if you think, even for a moment, that you should comfort the grieving woman in the dark, you will find no woman at all. All that you will find is death.

A Warning to All

To this day, villagers warn the unwary to never follow the sound of a crying woman into the jungle, nor to ever trust the beauty of a lone stranger on the path. Never stop walking if you hear a single, echoing footstep behind you, because La Patasola is always hunting. And once she has your scent, she will never stop until you are hers.

The Fugitive Prince

This story has been adapted from a tale originally told by Lewis Spence in The Myths Of Mexico & Peru, published in 1913 by Thomas Y. Crowell Company, New York. The Myths of Mexico & Peru provides an overview of the rich mythological traditions of these ancient civilizations, drawing upon archaeological evidence, historical accounts, and indigenous sources. Spence's work delves into various aspects of Mesoamerican and Andean cosmology, religion, rituals, deities, and legendary figures, offering insights into the cultural and spiritual beliefs of these societies.

The Fugitive Prince

Nezahualcoyotl, whose name means "Fasting Coyote," was the heir to the throne of Texcoco. He witnessed the brutal murder of his father from his hiding place in a nearby tree and barely managed to escape the invading forces. His dramatic journey to freedom has been compared to that of the Young Pretender, Prince Charles Edward Stuart, after the failed Jacobite uprising of 1745.

However, Nezahualcoyotl's freedom was short-lived. His pursuers soon captured him and dragged him back to his homeland, where he was thrown into prison. There, he found an unexpected ally in the local governor, who had once owed his position to the prince's late father. With the governor's help, Nezahualcoyotl escaped once again, slipping through the grasp of his enemies. But his saviour paid a heavy price, for the governor was executed for aiding him.

Seeking safety, Nezahualcoyotl turned to the Mexican royal family, who intervened on his behalf. He was granted asylum at the Aztec court, where he found temporary refuge. Eventually, he returned to his hometown of Texcoco and was allowed to stay in the very palace where his father had once ruled.

For the next eight years, he lived there in obscurity, surviving only through the reluctant generosity of the Tepanec ruler who had stolen his throne. Though unnoticed and powerless for the time being, he was biding his time, waiting for the moment to reclaim his birthright.

Maxtla the Fierce

Over time, the original Tecpanec conqueror passed away, and his son, Maxtla, took the throne. Unlike his father, Maxtla had no patience for Nezahualcoyotl, the scholarly prince who had travelled to the Tecpanec capital to pay his respects. Instead of welcoming him, Maxtla rejected his offer of friendship.

Sensing danger, a sympathetic courtier warned Nezahualcoyotl to flee for his safety. Taking the advice, the prince returned to Tezcuco, but Maxtla was already plotting against him. That evening, during a public event, the tyrant saw his opportunity to strike. However, Nezahualcoyotl's trusted teacher outsmarted the assassins by disguising a lookalike in the prince's place, allowing Nezahualcoyotl to escape unnoticed.

Furious at this failure, Maxtla sent an armed force to Tezcuco with orders to kill Nezahualcoyotl immediately. Once again, the prince's loyal protector discovered the plan and urged him to run. But this time, Nezahualcoyotl refused to flee, for he had made up his mind to stay and face his enemies.

A Romantic Escape

When they arrived, he was in the middle of playing tlachtli, the traditional Mexican ball game. With great politeness, he invited them inside and offered them food. As they ate, he excused himself and stepped into another room. His departure did not raise suspicion, as he remained visible through the open doorway that connected the rooms.

However, in the vestibule stood a large censer, releasing thick clouds of incense smoke. The rising smoke gradually obscured their view, making it difficult to see his movements. Taking advantage of the cover, he slipped into a hidden underground passage that led to an old, disused water pipe. Crawling through the pipe, he managed to escape unnoticed.

A Thrilling Pursuit

For a time, Nezahualcoyotl managed to evade capture by hiding in the home of a devoted supporter. His enemies searched the hut but failed to check beneath a pile of maguey fibre, used for making cloth, where he lay hidden. Furious that his rival had escaped, Maxtla intensified the hunt, launching a full-scale search of the countryside around Tezcuco. He offered a large reward for Nezahualcoyotl's capture, dead or alive, promising not only riches but also a noble estate and the hand of an aristocratic woman to anyone who turned him in.

With the pressure mounting, Nezahualcoyotl was forced to flee deep into the mountainous terrain between Tezcuco and Tlascala. He lived like an outcast, taking shelter in caves and dense forests, sneaking out only at night to scavenge for food. His nights were restless, always on the move to avoid detection. Pursued relentlessly, he was often forced to find clever hiding places to survive. On one occasion, friendly soldiers hid him inside a massive drum, and on another, a young woman covered him beneath chia stalks as she worked in the fields.

Despite the danger, the people of Tezcuco remained fiercely loyal to their rightful prince. Many of them endured torture and even death rather than reveal his location to Maxtla's men. Just when things seemed most hopeless, Nezahualcoyotl's luck began to turn. Maxtla's rule had become widely hated, and the people in the lands he had conquered were growing increasingly restless under his harsh and oppressive leadership. Change was on the horizon.

The Defeat of Maxtla

The rebels, determined to overthrow the tyrant, united against him and chose Nezahualcoyotl as their leader. He accepted the command, and in a decisive battle, they crushed the Tecpanec usurper.

With his rightful place restored, Nezahualcoyotl formed an alliance with Mexico, and with the help of its ruler, they defeated the last of Maxtla's forces. Maxtla was captured while hiding in the baths of Azcapotzalco, dragged out, and sacrificed. His city was then destroyed, bringing his reign to a definitive end.

The Solon of Anahuac

Nezahualcoyotl learned from the hardships he had faced and became a wise and just ruler. His legal code was strict, but his leadership was so fair and forward-thinking that he earned the title "The Solon of Anahuac," comparing him to the great Athenian lawmaker.

A strong supporter of the arts, he established a Council of Music to oversee and promote artistic expression in all its forms. Beyond his role as a ruler, he was likely Mexico's greatest native poet. One of his most famous odes, reflecting on the fleeting nature of life, reveals deep wisdom and closely mirrors the themes found in the poetry of Omar Khayyám.

The Queen with a Hundred Lovers

This story has also been adapted from a tale originally told by Lewis Spence in The Myths Of Mexico & Peru, published in 1913 by Thomas Y. Crowell Company, New York.

When King Axaiacatzin of Mexico and other noble lords sent their daughters to King Nezahualpilli so he could choose a queen whose son would inherit the throne, the most prestigious among them was Chachiuhnenetzin, the young daughter of the Mexican king. Raised in luxury, she lived in a separate palace with over two thousand attendants, as befitted her royal status.

However, despite her youth, Chachiuhnenetzin was both cunning and corrupt. She realized that those around her feared her power, and she abused her authority without restraint. Whenever she saw a young man she desired, she would secretly order him brought to her, and soon after, she would have him killed. She would then commission a statue in his likeness, decorating it with fine clothing, gold, and jewellery, and placing it in her chamber. Over time, the room filled with statues, each representing a life she had taken.

When King Nezahualpilli visited her and noticed the statues, she claimed they were her personal gods. Since the Mexicans were deeply devoted to their deities, he believed her and asked no further questions. But no crime remains hidden forever. Eventually, her secret was uncovered when three young men, Chicuhcoatl, Huitzilimitzin, and Maxtla, managed to survive. One of them, Maxtla, was a noble lord of Tesoyucan, while the other two were also of high rank.

One day, the king noticed a rare jewel on one of them, a jewel he had personally gifted to the queen. Though he did not immediately suspect betrayal, the sight unsettled him. That night, when he visited Chachiuhnenetzin's chamber, her attendants told him she was asleep, expecting him to leave as he had done before. However, the mystery of the jewel made him insist on entering. When he pulled back the covers, he found not his queen, but a statue made in her likeness, even adorned with her own hair.

Realizing something was terribly wrong, the king summoned his guards and household for a full search of the palace. Eventually, Chachiuhnenetzin was discovered at a feast with the three young nobles, all of whom were immediately arrested. The king ordered an investigation, which uncovered the full extent of her crimes. Testimonies from her servants revealed that many had helped her lure young men into the palace, others had sculpted the statues, and some had disposed of the bodies.

Once the case was clear, King Nezahualpilli sent official messengers to the rulers of Mexico and Tlacopan, informing them of what had happened and announcing the public execution of the queen and her accomplices. He also issued a decree summoning all lords, noblewomen, and even young girls across the empire to witness the punishment, ensuring it would serve as a powerful warning. In addition, he arranged a temporary truce with all of the empire's enemies, allowing them safe passage to see justice unfold.

When the day arrived, the city of Tezcuco was overwhelmed with people, struggling to contain the enormous crowd. Before all assembled, Chachiuhnenetzin and her three lovers were publicly executed by garrotte, a method of strangulation using a tightened rope. Because of their noble status, their bodies were burned alongside the statues she had kept.

But the punishments did not end there. More than two thousand people, servants, artisans, and others who had aided in her crimes, were also sentenced to death. They were executed and burned in a massive pit near a temple dedicated to the god of adultery.

The punishment was praised by all, except for the Mexican lords, her relatives, who were deeply angered by the humiliation of their royal family. Though they concealed their rage, they secretly plotted revenge.

According to the chronicler, this tragedy was not without irony, for Nezahualpilli himself was said to be paying for the sins of his father, who had once used deception to claim his mother as his wife. Thus, the curse had returned to his own household.

The Noble Tlascalan

This story has also been adapted from a tale originally told by Lewis Spence in The Myths Of Mexico & Peru, published in 1913 by Thomas Y. Crowell Company, New York.

In a society where human sacrifice was common, many stories arose about those who met this grim fate. One of the most remarkable is the tale of Tlalhuicole, a noble warrior from Tlaxcala, who was captured in battle by the forces of Montezuma, the emperor of the Aztecs.

Less than a year before the Spanish arrived in Mexico, war erupted between the Huexotzincans and the Tlaxcalans, with the Aztecs siding with the Huexotzincans. In the heat of battle, the Aztecs managed to capture Tlalhuicole through deception, a feat in itself, as he was such a formidable warrior that the mere mention of his name struck fear into even the bravest Mexican fighters.

He was taken to Tenochtitlán in a cage and presented to Montezuma, who, upon realizing who he was, did something extraordinary: instead of sentencing him to death, he set him free and showered him with honours and gifts. In an even more unusual gesture, Montezuma offered him the chance to return home, something he had never done for any other captive.

But Tlalhuicole refused his freedom. Instead, he insisted that he should be sacrificed to the gods, as was customary for captured warriors. Montezuma, who deeply respected him, could not bring himself to allow this.

At that moment, war broke out between the Aztecs and the Tarascans, and Montezuma, seeing an opportunity, appointed Tlalhuicole as the commander of his forces. Tlalhuicole accepted the position, led the Aztecs into battle, and crushed the Tarascans, returning to Tenochtitlán with great wealth and many prisoners. The entire city celebrated his victory, and Montezuma once again urged him to stay and become a citizen of Mexico.

But Tlalhuicole remained loyal to his homeland. He refused to betray Tlaxcala and declined Montezuma's offer of freedom as well, saying he could not live with the shame of having been defeated and captured. Instead, he pleaded for death, asking to be sacrificed so he could die the honourable death of a warrior.

Montezuma, himself a man of honour, understood and respected his wish. He agreed and ordered Tlalhuicole to face his final test, the gladiatorial combat at the temalacatl, the bloodstained stone of sacrifice.

The greatest Aztec warriors were sent to fight him, and Montezuma himself watched the battle. Tlalhuicole fought like a lion, killing eight elite warriors and injuring more than twenty, but in the end, he was overwhelmed, his body covered in wounds.

The priests seized him, dragging him to the altar of Huitzilopochtli, the god of war. There, in front of the assembled crowd, his heart was cut from his chest, offered to the gods as the final act of a warrior's life.

Tlalhuicole had met his end not as a captive, but as a true warrior, embracing the only fate he believed worthy of his honour.

Legend Of The Callejón Del Muerto

This story has been adapted from a tale originally told by Thomas A. Janvier in Legends Of The City Of Mexico, published in 1910 by Harper & Brothers Publishers, New York. Legends of the City of Mexico delves into the rich cultural heritage of Mexico, exploring the myths and legends that have been passed down through generations. The book included a diverse range of stories, drawing from Aztec, Spanish, and indigenous Mexican traditions.

It is both unwise and wrong, Señor, to make a vow to the Blessed Virgin, or to even the smallest saint in the calendar, and then fail to keep it, especially when the Virgin or saint has done exactly what was asked of them. This is something that Don Tristan de Alculer learned the hard way. When he died without fulfilling his promise, he found himself unable to enjoy the peace of heaven among the angels. Instead, he was forced to make good on his vow after death, something he could and should have done while he was still alive.

Don Tristan de Alculer was a humble but honourable Spanish merchant who had travelled from the Philippines to Mexico City to make a new life for himself. He arrived during the rule of Viceroy Marqués de Villa Manrique, a man deeply invested in expanding trade with the East. Unfortunately, this increased commerce also attracted the attention of English pirates, none more infamous than Sir Francis Drake, who managed to seize a Spanish galleon so weighed down with silver and gold that it was nearly sinking.

Don Tristan, already an older man, had come with his son, also named Tristan, to help him establish his trade. The younger Tristan was an intelligent and capable businessman, but the family arrived in Mexico City with very little money. Their humble beginnings led them to settle in a small, nameless alley so poor and forgotten that no one had ever bothered to give it a proper name. It was only after Don Tristan's broken vow that the street came to be known as "The Alley of the Dead Man."

Despite their modest means, Don Tristan and his son were respected members of the community, as proven by their close friendship with the Archbishop himself, Don Fray García de Santa María Mendoza. Don Tristan the elder often sought his counsel on spiritual matters, which makes his eventual mistake all the more tragic.

Years passed, and their business began to thrive. Then, one fateful season, Tristan the younger travelled to the coast to purchase goods. Unfortunately, he arrived during the worst time of year, when deadly fevers swept through the region. He fell gravely ill, so much so that it seemed his feet were already halfway through death's door.

In his desperation, Don Tristan the elder made a solemn vow to the Blessed Virgin of Guadalupe. He promised that if she spared his son's life, he would walk barefoot from his home to her Sanctuary and there, at her altar, offer his deepest gratitude.

The Blessed Virgin, full of love and compassion, heard his prayer and took pity on him. She kept her end of the bargain, and the fever vanished, and young Tristan returned home, alive and well.

But Don Tristan, having received what he asked for, would soon forget the price of an unfulfilled promise…

Don Tristan had received everything he had prayed for from the Blessed Virgin, but when it came time to fulfil his promise to her, he hesitated. By then, he was an old man, plagued by rheumatism, and the idea of walking three miles barefoot filled him with dread.

At first, he told himself he would do it in a week or two, believing the Blessed Virgin wouldn't mind the delay. Then he postponed it again. And again. Every time he thought about walking barefoot on the cold earth, his feet shivered, and his legs trembled at the thought of making his condition worse. And so, time passed, and the Blessed Virgin never got what was rightfully hers.

But Don Tristan couldn't shake the unease in his soul. He knew he was breaking his word, and it gnawed at him. Hoping for a way out, he turned to his friend, the Archbishop, expecting that, as a favour, he might release him from his vow.

Now, Señor, I must say, I don't believe the Archbishop made the wisest decision in this matter. Despite his high position and his authority in spiritual affairs, his response was a little too lenient. He reassured Don Tristan that the Blessed Virgin was too compassionate to hold him to a promise that could leave him bedridden, or worse, dead. Given Don Tristan's frail state, forcing himself to walk such a distance could be dangerous. And so, being a kind and easy-going man, the Archbishop absolved him of his vow.

But a vow is a vow, Señor, and not even an Archbishop has the power to undo it. And that was made very clear, very quickly.

Because while the Blessed Virgin is patient and not easily offended, she does not stand idly by when her rightful dues are ignored. And when she is truly angered, she acts swiftly.

Just three days after Don Tristan received his dispensation, one that, as it turned out, he should never have been granted, the Archbishop set out on the twelfth of the month to perform Mass at the Villa de Guadalupe in Our Lady's Sanctuary, following long-held tradition.

After the service, as he rode back to the city on his mule, he was met with a terrifying sight. Don Tristan was walking toward him, his face deathly pale, his feet bare. The Archbishop's mule froze in fear, trembling beneath him, as Don Tristan stopped briefly, reached out, and grasped his hand. The touch of his skin was icy cold.

Then, in a hollow, eerie voice, Don Tristan spoke. "For the sake of my soul, I am fulfilling my vow to Our Lady. I have come to understand that if I fail to do so, I will burn in Hell for all eternity!"

Without another word, he turned and walked away slowly and painfully toward Our Lady's shrine, never looking back.

The Archbishop was overcome with fear, just as his mule was. When the animal finally regained enough composure to move, he rode straight to Don Tristan's house, though in his heart, he already knew what he would find there.

And indeed, he found exactly what he had dreaded.

Inside the house, Don Tristan lay dead, his lifeless body stretched out on the bed, surrounded by four flickering death candles. His hands were clasped together on his chest, a black funeral pall draped over him. His death-pale face bore the same expression as when he had passed the Archbishop on the road.

Seeing this, the Archbishop shivered violently, his teeth chattering in his skull. Everyone in the room, realizing they had witnessed something beyond human understanding, fell to their knees in reverence and fear, offering prayers for Don Tristan's soul.

But, perhaps their prayers were not enough. Or maybe Don Tristan's broken vow was so grave that he was sentenced to spend a long time in Purgatory before he could find peace.

Either way, it soon became clear that Don Tristan had not entirely left the world of the living.

Not long after his death, people began seeing him wandering the streets at midnight. Wrapped in a long, flowing white shroud, he carried a huge candle that burned with a yellow, ghostly light. He walked the same street he had lived on for so many years, pacing up and down in the dead of night. Those unfortunate enough to encounter him fled in terror.

In time, every last resident abandoned the street, leaving it deserted. And so, it became known as the Alley of the Dead Man, Callejón del Muerto.

Even now, more than three hundred years later, many claim that Don Tristan's spirit still lingers. My friend, the cargador, along with several other reliable witnesses, swears that his ghost can still be seen at midnight, carrying his flaming candle and marching through the empty street.

As for me? I wouldn't dare walk down the Callejón del Muerto at midnight, even today.

The Return of Papantzin

This story has been adapted from a tale originally told by Lewis Spence in The Myths Of Mexico & Peru, published in 1913 by Thomas Y. Crowell Company, New York.

When Montezuma ascended the throne, he arranged the marriage of Papantzin to one of his most esteemed officials, the governor of Tlatelulco. After her husband's passing, Papantzin continued to exercise his near viceregal authority and resided in his palace.

In time, she too passed away, and her funeral was attended by the emperor himself, alongside the most distinguished members of his court and kingdom. Her body was laid to rest in an underground tomb within the palace grounds, near the royal baths, which were secluded within the vast gardens of the residence. The entrance to the vault was sealed with a stone slab, and once all the required funeral rites for a royal figure had been completed, the emperor and his entourage departed.

At daybreak the following morning, one of the royal children, a six-year-old girl, wandered into the garden searching for her governess.

To her astonishment, she saw Princess Papantzin standing near the baths. Recognising her aunt, the girl ran to tell her governess, who dismissed her words as childish imagination. However, when the girl insisted, the governess reluctantly followed her into the garden, only to see Papantzin herself, sitting on one of the steps leading to the baths. The shock overwhelmed the woman, and she collapsed in a faint.

The child, now alarmed, hurried to her mother's chamber and explained what had happened. The mother, accompanied by two attendants, rushed to the baths and was struck with fear at the sight of Papantzin. However, the princess quickly reassured her and requested to be taken to her rooms, urging her sister-in-law to keep the event a complete secret for the time being.

Later that day, Papantzin summoned Tiçotzicatzin, her major-domo, instructing him to inform Montezuma that she needed to see him immediately on a matter of utmost importance. Terrified by the request, the man hesitated, refusing to carry out the task. Papantzin then ordered that her uncle, Nezahualpilli, King of Tezcuco, be summoned instead. Upon receiving the urgent message, Nezahualpilli hurried to the palace, where Papantzin implored him to speak with the emperor without delay and persuade him to come at once.

When Montezuma heard his uncle's account, he was shocked and doubtful. However, he quickly made his way to his sister, exclaiming as he approached, "Is it truly you, my sister, or some malevolent spirit taking your form?"

"It is I, your Majesty," she answered calmly.

Montezuma, still astounded, sat down with the high-ranking nobles who had accompanied him. A hush of expectation fell over the gathering as Papantzin began to speak:

"Listen carefully to what I am about to reveal. You saw me dead and buried, yet now you see me alive once more. By the authority of our ancestors, my brother, I have returned from the land of the dead to deliver a prophecy of great importance…

"At the moment of my death, I found myself in a vast valley with no clear beginning or end, surrounded by towering mountains. In the middle of the valley, I came across a road that split into many different paths. A great river ran along the edge of the valley, its waters roaring as they flowed.

"By the riverbank, I saw a young man dressed in a long robe, fastened with a diamond and shining as brightly as the sun. His face glowed like a star, and on his forehead was a cross-shaped mark. He had wings, their feathers shimmering with brilliant colours, and his eyes gleamed like emeralds. His expression was both powerful and gentle.

"He took me by the hand and said, 'Come with me. It is not yet your time to cross the river. You have the love of God within you, greater than you can understand.'

"He then led me through the valley, where I saw countless skulls and bones of the dead. Ahead, I noticed a group of dark-skinned figures, horned and with the hooves of deer. They were constructing a house, nearly complete. As I turned eastward, I saw an immense fleet of ships on the river, manned by a great number of men who looked different from us. Their eyes were a clear grey, their skin was ruddy, and they carried banners and standards in their hands. They wore helmets upon their heads and called themselves the 'Sons of the Sun.'

"The radiant young man guiding me explained that it was not yet the will of the gods for me to cross the river. Instead, I was to return and witness the future with my own eyes, to benefit from the faith that these strangers would bring. He told me that the bones scattered across the plain belonged to our people, who had died in ignorance of this faith and had suffered greatly because of it. The house being built by the dark figures was meant for those who would fall in battle against the seafaring strangers. My purpose was to return to my people, to tell them of the true faith and to warn them of what was to come so they might prepare."

Montezuma listened in silence, deeply troubled by what he had heard. Without a word, he left his sister's presence and returned to his private chambers, lost in dark and heavy thoughts.

The resurrection of Princess Papantzin is one of the most well-documented events in Mexican history. It is remarkable that, upon the arrival of the Spanish Conquistadors, one of the first to embrace Christianity and receive baptism was none other than Princess Papantzin herself.

The Legend Of the Dwarf

This story has been adapted from a tale originally told by Lewis Spence in The Myths Of Mexico & Peru, published in 1913 by Thomas Y. Crowell Company, New York.

There was once an old woman who lived alone in her hut, rarely leaving her place by the fire. She longed desperately for a child, and in her sorrow, she took an egg, wrapped it carefully in cotton cloth, and placed it in a corner of her home. Each day, she checked it anxiously, but nothing changed. Then, one morning, she discovered the shell had cracked open, and inside was a tiny, beautiful creature reaching out to her.

The old woman was overjoyed. She took the little being to her heart, arranged for a nurse to care for him, and looked after him so well that, by the end of a year, the child could walk and speak as fluently as an adult. However, he never grew any bigger. But the woman was so proud of him that she declared he would one day become a great leader.

One day, she told him to go to the king's palace and challenge him to a test of strength. The dwarf begged her not to send him on such a mission, but she insisted, and so he had no choice but to obey. When he arrived at the royal court, he issued his challenge. The king, amused by the tiny challenger, set him a task to lift a stone weighing three arobes (75lb.).

The dwarf returned home in tears, but his mother sent him straight back, saying, 'If the king can lift the stone, then you can too.'

Sure enough, the king lifted the heavy stone, but so too did the dwarf. The king then set him many other trials, but no matter what feats of strength he performed, the dwarf matched him every time. Frustrated at being bested by such a small creature, the king set him a final, impossible challenge. Unless the dwarf built a palace taller than any in the city, he would be put to death.

Terrified, the dwarf ran back to his mother. She comforted him and told him not to despair. The next morning, both of them awoke inside a magnificent palace, one that still stands to this day.

When the king saw this astonishing sight, he sent for the dwarf again. This time, he challenged him to a brutal test. Each of them would collect a bundle of cogoiol (a kind of hardwood), and the king would strike the dwarf on the head with his bundle first. If the dwarf survived, he would be allowed to strike back.

Once again, the child ran home, sobbing. But his mother reassured him. She placed a tortilla on his head and sent him back to face the king. In front of the gathered nobles, the king struck the dwarf repeatedly, but the bundle broke apart, leaving him completely unharmed. Seeing this, the king tried to withdraw from the challenge, afraid of what would happen when the dwarf had his turn.

But he had already made a vow in front of his court, and he could not go back on his word.

The dwarf struck him once, then twice, and on the second blow, the king's skull shattered. The watching nobles immediately declared the dwarf their new ruler.

After this, the old woman vanished.

But in the village of Maní, fifty miles away, there is a deep well that leads to a subterranean passage stretching all the way to Mérida. In this passage, an old woman sits by the riverbank, shaded by a great tree, with a serpent at her side. She offers water to travellers, but she does not accept money. Instead, she demands something far more terrible. She asks for innocent children, who are devoured by the serpent.

They say this old woman is the dwarf's mother.

Vukub-Cakix, the Great Macaw

This story has been adapted from a tale originally told by Lewis Spence in The Myths Of Mexico & Peru, published in 1913 by Thomas Y. Crowell Company, New York.

Vukub-Cakix, the Great Macaw

Before the earth had fully recovered from the great flood that had devastated it, there lived a proud and arrogant being named Vukub-Cakix, which translates to "Seven-Times-the-Colour-of-Fire", a reference to the brilliant plumage of the great macaw. His teeth were made of emerald, and his body shimmered with gold and silver, marking him as a deity associated with the sun and moon in ancient times. However, his arrogance and constant boasting angered the gods, who decided he must be destroyed.

Vukub-Cakix had two sons, Zipacna and Cabrakan, one known as Earth-Heaper, the other as Earthquake. These brothers were also filled with pride and defiance. To put an end to their reign, the gods sent the heavenly twins, Hun-Apu and Xbalanque, down to earth with the task of humbling them.

Vukub-Cakix took great pride in his nanze tree, the tapal, which bore round, golden, fragrant fruit. Every morning, he climbed to its top to pick the ripest fruit for his breakfast. But one morning, as he reached the summit, he was enraged to find two strangers had arrived before him and had nearly stripped the tree bare.

Before he could react, Hun-Apu raised a blowpipe and fired a dart straight into his mouth. The giant fell from the tree, crashing to the ground in agony. Seizing the opportunity, Hun-Apu leapt down to restrain him, but Vukub-Cakix, in his fury, wrenched Hun-Apu's arm from his body.

Wounded and furious, Vukub-Cakix staggered back to his home, where his wife, Chimalmat, rushed to his side, asking what had happened. Pointing to his injured mouth, he roared in pain. Believing he had taken his revenge by stealing Hun-Apu's arm, he hung the severed limb over a fire, while cursing the intruders who had dared to challenge him.

While Vukub-Cakix groaned and howled in agony, his wife slowly turned Hun-Apu's arm over the flames, basting it carefully. The god, sensing the poisonous dart was tormenting him, swore vengeance against those who had brought him such suffering.

But Hun-Apu and Xbalanque were not about to let him escape so easily. Determined to recover the stolen arm, they sought the help of two wise and ancient magicians, Xpiyacoc and Xmucane, who were among the original creators of the world. These elders advised them to disguise themselves and accompany them to Vukub-Cakix's house, posing as healers.

When they arrived at Vukub-Cakix's mansion, they could hear his cries of pain from far away. Stepping inside, they introduced themselves as famous doctors who had come to offer their healing skills.

Vukub-Cakix was suspicious at first and demanded to know the identities of the two young men accompanying them.

"They are our sons," the magicians replied.

"Very well," said Vukub-Cakix. "Can you cure me?"

"Without a doubt," assured Xpiyacoc. "You have suffered severe injuries to your mouth and eyes."

Vukub-Cakix groaned. "It was demons with a blowpipe who did this to me! If you can heal me, I will reward you handsomely."

The old magician nodded. "Your Highness, your teeth are badly damaged and must be removed. Also, your eyes appear to be infected."

At this, Vukub-Cakix grew alarmed, but the magicians calmed him with sweet words.

"Fear not," Xpiyacoc said. "We will replace your teeth with grains of maize, which are much more suitable."

Trusting the healers, Vukub-Cakix agreed to the procedure. With careful precision, Xpiyacoc and Xmucane removed his emerald teeth and replaced them with simple grains of white maize. Instantly, the giant lost his brilliance, and his shimmering gold and silver faded. When the magicians removed his eyes, he collapsed into unconsciousness and died.

At the same time, Chimalmat was still turning Hun-Apu's arm over the fire, unaware of what had happened. Hun-Apu rushed forward, grabbed his arm, and reattached it with the help of the magicians.

With Vukub-Cakix defeated, the group left his house victorious, their mission complete.

The Earth-Giants

However, the mission was only partially completed, as Vukub's two sons, Zipacna and Cabrakan, were still at large. Zipacna spent his days raising mountains, while his brother, Cabrakan, shook the land with earthquakes. Determined to finish what they had started, Hun-Apu and Xbalanque set their sights on Zipacna first, plotting with a group of young men to bring about his downfall.

The young men, four hundred in total, pretended to be building a house. They cut down a massive tree, claiming it was to be the main support beam for their new home, and positioned themselves in a section of the forest where they knew Zipacna would pass.

Before long, they heard the thundering crash of trees being pushed aside, for Zipacna was approaching. When he caught sight of them standing helplessly around the enormous tree trunk, he found their struggle amusing.

"What have you there, little ones?" he asked with a chuckle.

"Just a tree, your Highness," they replied. "We have cut it down for the roof of a house we are building."

"Can't you lift it?" the giant scoffed.

"No, your Highness," they answered. "It's far too heavy, even with all of us combined."

Laughing, Zipacna bent down, hoisted the tree onto his shoulder with ease, and told them to lead the way. He followed without a hint of strain, completely unaware of the trap that awaited him.

The young men, under Hun-Apu and Xbalanque's instructions, had dug a deep pit, claiming it was to be the foundation of their house. When they asked Zipacna to lower the trunk inside, he obliged without hesitation. As soon as he reached the bottom, they hurled enormous logs down on top of him, believing they had crushed him to death.

Certain that the giant was dead, they celebrated immediately, singing and dancing with joy. To make their deception even more convincing, Zipacna sent out ants carrying strands of his hair. When the young men saw them, they took it as proof of his demise. Satisfied with their victory, they continued building their house atop the logs they thought had buried their foe, and soon enough, they were drinking pulque and feasting in triumph. The night filled with laughter and revelry.

But below them, Zipacna lay hidden, waiting for his moment of revenge.

Then, with the sudden force of a raging storm, he erupted from the earth, hurling the entire house and everyone inside it into the air. The dwelling was obliterated, and the four hundred young men were thrown skyward with such force that they never returned.

To this day, their fate remains unchanged, for in the cluster of stars we call the Pleiades, they can still be seen, endlessly waiting for their chance to come back down to earth.

The Undoing of Zipacna

Hun-Apu and Xbalanque, saddened by the loss of their comrades, decided that Zipacna could not be allowed to escape so easily. By night, he carried mountains, and by day, he searched for food along the riverbank, catching fish and crabs.

The brothers devised a clever trap. They created a large artificial crab and placed it inside a cavern at the bottom of a ravine. Then, they secretly weakened the foundations of a massive mountain and waited for Zipacna to arrive.

Before long, they spotted him walking along the river and called out to him. "Where are you headed?" they asked.

"Just searching for my daily food," Zipacna replied.

"And what does that consist of?"

"Only fish and crabs," said the giant.

The brothers exchanged knowing looks. "There's a huge crab down in that ravine," they said, pointing toward the cavern. "We saw it on our way here. It's truly enormous! More than enough to make you a fine breakfast."

Zipacna's eyes lit up. "Fantastic! I must have it at once!"

With a single leap, he bounded down into the ravine, heading straight for the cleverly placed crab. The moment he reached it, Hun-Apu and Xbalanque sent the mountain crashing down upon him. But even under the enormous weight of earth and rock, Zipacna struggled fiercely to free himself. Fearing that he might escape, the brothers ensured his fate by turning him to stone.

And so, at the foot of Mount Meahuan, near Vera Paz, the proud Mountain-Maker met his end.

The Discomfiture of Cabrakan

Now, only one of the boastful brothers remained, and he was the most arrogant of them all.

"I am the Overturner of Mountains!" he declared.

But Hun-Apu and Xbalanque had already decided that none of the Vukub bloodline would be left alive. At the very moment they were planning Cabrakan's downfall, he was busy moving mountains, grabbing them by their bases and hurling them into the sky with his immense strength. The smaller mountains weren't even worth his attention.

As he worked, he encountered the two brothers, who greeted him warmly. "Good day, Cabrakan," they said. "What are you doing?"

"Bah! Nothing at all," the giant scoffed. "Can't you see? I'm tossing mountains around, as I always do. And who are you to ask such foolish questions? What are your names?"

"We don't have names," they replied. "We're just hunters, using our blowpipes to catch birds in these mountains. We don't need names, we meet no one."

Cabrakan sneered at them, ready to move on, but they stopped him.

"Wait," they said. "We'd love to see your strength in action. Show us how you throw mountains!"

His pride was too great to resist.

"Very well," he boasted. "Tell me which mountain you want me to destroy, and before you know it, I'll have turned it to dust."

Hun-Apu scanned the horizon and pointed at a towering peak.

"What about that one? Do you think you can bring it down?"

Cabrakan laughed loudly. "Easily!" he bragged. "Let's go!"

But Hun-Apu stopped him. "Wait," he said. "You haven't eaten all day, and such a great feat shouldn't be attempted on an empty stomach."

Cabrakan's eyes lit up with hunger. "You're right," he said eagerly. Cabrakan was always hungry. "But what do you have for me?"

"Nothing," Hun-Apu admitted.

Cabrakan's temper flared. "What a joke!" he roared. "You ask me what I want to eat, only to tell me you have nothing?" In his fury, he grabbed a small mountain and flung it into the sea, sending waves crashing into the sky.

"Calm down," Hun-Apu said. "Don't get angry. We'll hunt a bird for you with our blowpipes."

Hearing this, Cabrakan's rage cooled slightly. "Why didn't you say so before?" he grumbled. "Be quick about it, I'm starving."

Just then, a large bird flew overhead. The brothers took aim, and their darts struck true. The bird fell to the ground at Cabrakan's feet.

"Incredible!" the giant exclaimed. "You two are skilled hunters indeed!" He snatched up the bird, ready to devour it raw.

But Hun-Apu stopped him. "Wait," he said. "It will taste much better cooked."

He rubbed two sticks together to start a fire, while Xbalanque gathered wood. Soon, flames blazed brightly, and they placed the bird over the fire to roast.

As it cooked, a delicious aroma filled the air, making Cabrakan's mouth water. But what the giant didn't know was that Hun-Apu had coated the bird in a layer of poisoned mud, a deadly mineral called tizate, which seeped into the meat as it cooked.

When it was ready, the brothers handed the bird to Cabrakan, who devoured it without hesitation.

"Now," said Hun-Apu, "let's see if you can move that mountain as you claimed."

But something was wrong. Cabrakan felt a strange pain in his stomach. "What's happening?" he muttered, wiping sweat from his brow. "I can't seem to see the mountain properly."

"Nonsense," Hun-Apu said. "It's right there, to the east."

"My vision is blurry," Cabrakan groaned.

"No, no," Hun-Apu taunted. "You said you could move mountains, and now you're just making excuses!"

"I swear, something is wrong," Cabrakan mumbled, swaying unsteadily. "Take me to the mountain!"

"Of course," Hun-Apu said, leading him forward. Within moments, they stood at the foot of the towering peak.

"Go on, then," Hun-Apu said mockingly. "Let's see you lift it."

Cabrakan stared blankly at the massive rock before him. His legs trembled so violently that they sounded like war drums, and sweat poured down his face, running in rivulets down the mountainside.

"Well?" Hun-Apu jeered. "Are you going to move it or not?"

"He can't," Xbalanque smirked. "I knew he couldn't."

Cabrakan shook himself, trying desperately to regain his strength, but it was too late. The poison had spread through his veins. With one last groan, he collapsed, dead at the brothers' feet.

And so, the last of the earth giants of Guatemala was destroyed, just as Hun-Apu and Xbalanque had been sent to do.

The Giant Pyramid-Builder

This story has been adapted from a tale originally told by Henry Wysham Lanier in A Book Of Giants, published in 1922 by E. P. Dutton & Company, New York. A Book of Giants presents a series of tales featuring giants from various cultures and mythologies around the world. Giants have long been a fascinating subject in folklore and mythology, often depicted as powerful and monstrous beings with immense strength and size. Lanier's collection gathers together stories from different traditions, offering readers a glimpse into the rich tapestry of giant lore.

For 4,800 years after the world was created, the land of Anahuac was inhabited by a race of giants. These massive beings were the sworn enemies of both gods and men. The people of Tlascala fought relentless wars against them, and although many giants were eventually overwhelmed or driven into the wilderness to starve, there were always enough left to plunge the land into turmoil.

Among the most powerful and defiant were Xelhua and his six brothers. They ignored all laws, lived by their own cruel and merciless desires, and terrorised the land with their great strength and cunning. Their arrogance grew unchecked, believing that neither god nor mortal could challenge their will.

At last, the gods could stand it no longer. They decided to wipe out the giants once and for all and unleashed a cataclysmic flood upon the world.

The skies split open, releasing endless torrents of rain, while the oceans surged beyond their shores, swallowing entire lands. Underground rivers erupted through the earth, flooding everything in their path. Giants and humans alike perished, and those who did not drown were transformed into fish.

Only Xelhua and his brothers survived. As the waters rose, they fled north and took refuge in the caves of Mount Tlaloc. They sealed themselves inside, rolling enormous boulders across the entrances to keep out the floodwaters. Safe in their hidden sanctuary, they waited for the storm to pass.

When the waters finally receded, the gods withdrew their punishment, and the flood returned to its place in the clouds, the earth, and the sea.

Xelhua and his brothers emerged from their caves, now the only living beings left. Using their skills, they repopulated the earth, creating a new race of humans, destined to serve them.

Surviving the flood only made Xelhua even more arrogant. Had he not outwitted the wrath of the gods? Now he decided to build a monument so grand that it would serve both as a symbol of his triumph and a means of escape should the gods try to destroy him again.

On the plains of Cholula, he ordered the construction of an enormous pyramid, so vast that it would pierce the clouds.

In Tlamanalco, at the foot of the Sierra, thousands of workers were put to work, digging clay, shaping bricks, and burning them in kilns. To speed up the process, Xelhua created a human chain stretching from the brickyard to Cholula, so that bricks could be passed from hand to hand, ensuring the builders never ran out of materials. Bitumen was also transported from distant lands to reinforce the bricks and keep the pyramid strong.

Day by day, the incredible structure grew taller, its massive foundations rising as if they were alive. Even Xelhua himself struggled to climb to its highest levels, where his workers laboured like ants, placing brick after brick.

But pride breeds greed, and looking upon his work, Xelhua regretted not making the base even bigger. Surely the only thing limiting his creation was space itself. No matter, once this pyramid reached the heavens, he would build another even greater, ensuring that no future flood could ever reach him.

But the gods do not sleep, even when they are silent. They watched in fury as the pyramid grew, its arrogant builder defying their power. Yet they waited, allowing it to rise higher and higher, until the clouds often lay beneath its peak.

Then, on the day when the final phase of construction was in sight, Xelhua pushed his workers harder than ever. The pyramid was almost complete. At that moment, the heavens opened once more. A massive flaming boulder fell from the sky, smashing into the pyramid with unstoppable force. The top section collapsed, crushing thousands of workers beneath the rubble, including Xelhua himself.

From that day forward, no one doubted the power of the gods. The ruins of the pyramid were dedicated to the god Quetzalcoatl, and for generations, priests told the tale of Xelhua's downfall.

Even in the time of the Dominican friar Pedro de los Rios, people still pointed to a strange, toad-shaped stone, believed to be a fragment of the very thunderbolt that had brought the pyramid down.

And so, Xelhua's mad ambition was forever remembered in song and festival, warning all who heard it to respect the gods. Furthermore, from that day onward, humanity no longer spoke a single tongue. Instead, each tribe was given its own language, making them strangers to one another, as a reminder that no mortal could ever again challenge the divine.

El Duende

This story is my own adaptation of a traditional regional tale. This version of the tale was largely informed by sources from Guatemala.

The heart of the forest pulsed with a quiet, ancient rhythm. The canopy, dense and impenetrable to all but the faintest specks of light, filtered the world into hues of emerald and gold. Here, where the roots of the trees twisted into the earth like veins and the air hummed with the songs of unseen birds, lived a creature neither wholly of this world nor entirely beyond it.

A gnome, some whispered. A spirit, others claimed. To the travellers who chanced upon him, he was an enigma, mischief wrapped in shadow, a fleeting blur between the trees, a hushed giggle carried by the wind.

Small in stature, yet vibrant in presence, El Duende wore a pointed hat the colour of ripe berries and a coat woven from moss and lichen. His beard, wild and silvery as a river's reflection, trailed down to his chest, where it tangled in tiny trinkets of the forest, fallen feathers, smooth stones, and the occasional shimmering beetle that made a temporary home there. He was as much a part of the woodland as the whispering leaves and the murmuring brooks.

He thrived on mischief, delighting in riddles and pranks, yet never with malice. He would tie bootlaces together while their owners rested against the trunks of trees, leaving them to stumble with a surprised laugh. He plucked arrows from the quivers of hunters and replaced them with twigs, sending their quarry into the depths unharmed. The forest was his realm, and though it bowed to no master, it was, in a way, his to guard.

One evening, as twilight stretched its indigo fingers across the sky, a traveller stumbled through the undergrowth. He was young, weary, and cloaked in the dust of his long journey. His name was Juan, and he had wandered too far from the safety of his path. The trees whispered around him, their voices rustling in a language older than men, and the scent of damp earth and blooming night jasmine filled his lungs.

As Juan moved forward, the world around him changed. The underbrush grew thicker, the trees taller, and the familiar sounds of the forest, chirping crickets, the hoots of owls, became hushed, as if listening. Then there was the sound of laughter. It was light, musical, and teasing. It came from nowhere and everywhere at once. Juan turned sharply, his heart thudding, his pulse quickening. His eyes darted between the trees, searching for the source.

"Who's there?" he called, his voice swallowed by the vastness of the woods.

Again, the laughter, now closer, more playful. And then a flicker of movement just beyond sight. A glimpse of red darting between the tree trunks, then vanishing like mist before the morning sun.

"El Duende," he whispered, remembering the stories told in hushed voices over campfires.

A rustling from above drew his gaze. There, perched on a low-hanging branch, was a small figure, his feet dangling lazily. His eyes, bright and knowing, gleamed beneath the brim of his hat. He grinned, mischief curling at the edges of his lips.

"Lost, are we?" El Duende's voice was smooth, with an undertone of laughter.

Juan swallowed, torn between fascination and apprehension. "I... I only seek the way out."

El Duende tilted his head, considering the traveller. "Ah, the way out! Such a simple thing. And yet, what if it is not the way you should be seeking?"

Juan furrowed his brows. "What do you mean?"

El Duende hopped from the branch with impossible grace, landing with barely a whisper of movement. "You search for roads, paths carved by men. But the forest does not yield to such things." He stepped closer, the air around him alive with the scent of damp moss and wildflowers. "Perhaps what you truly need is something different."

Juan hesitated. "I need to go home."

"Home." El Duende mused, tapping his bearded chin. "A strange word, that. But very well! I shall help you, if you can keep up."

Without another word, he darted into the trees, his laughter trailing behind him like a ribbon in the wind. Juan had no choice but to follow.

Through the labyrinth of the jungle they ran, past towering ferns and silent pools where the moon cast silver reflections. The forest changed around them, shifting in ways Juan could not understand. One moment, they passed beneath vines heavy with glowing blossoms; the next, they ran across stepping stones that shimmered like glass. Time became meaningless, the journey a dream painted in shades of moonlight and shadow.

At last, just as Juan's breath grew ragged and his legs threatened to give way, they emerged into a clearing. The trees parted like sentinels bowing before a king, revealing the open landscape beyond.

El Duende turned, his eyes glinting with some ancient knowledge. "And so, your path lies ahead."

Juan followed his gaze. There, in the distance, lay the faint glow of torches, the unmistakable shape of rooftops against the darkened sky. It was his village. Relief flooded through him.

He turned back to thank El Duende, but the forest spirit was already retreating into the shadows, his form blending with the foliage. Only his voice remained, a whisper carried by the wind.

"Never lose your sense of wonder, traveller. It is the key to seeing beyond what is, to what might be."

And then he was gone.

Juan stood there for a moment, gazing into the forest, before finally stepping forward toward home. Yet something inside him had changed. The world no longer felt quite the same. The trees seemed to breathe, the stars above pulsed with a quiet rhythm, and the air itself carried the echoes of laughter.

Perhaps, he thought, as he crossed into the familiar paths of his village, El Duende had been right all along.

Legend Of Don Juan Manuel

This story has been adapted from a tale originally told by Thomas A. Janvier in Legends Of The City Of Mexico, published in 1910 by Harper & Brothers Publishers, New York. Legends of the City of Mexico delves into the rich cultural heritage of Mexico, exploring the myths and legends that have been passed down through generations. The book included a diverse range of stories, drawing from Aztec, Spanish, and indigenous Mexican traditions.

Don Juan Manuel was a wealthy and respected gentleman, but he had one dark vice. He took pleasure in killing people.

Every night, at eleven o'clock, as the Palace clock struck the hour, he would leave his grand home, which still stands today on the street that bears his name, wrapped in his heavy cloak, a dagger concealed beneath it.

He would walk through the dark, empty streets until he met someone. Then, in a polite tone, he would ask, "What time is it?"

If the unfortunate passerby had heard the clock chime, they would reply, "It is eleven o'clock at night."

To which Don Juan Manuel would answer, "Señor, you are the luckiest of men, for you know the exact hour of your death!"

With that, he would plunge his dagger into their heart, leaving the lifeless body behind, and return home as if nothing had happened.

This gruesome ritual continued for years.

Don Juan Manuel lived with his beloved nephew, with whom he shared supper every evening. After their meal, the nephew would often go out to visit friends, while Don Juan Manuel would set off to find his next victim.

But one night, the nephew did not return home.

Don Juan Manuel became uneasy, worried for his safety.

At dawn, the city watch came knocking on his door, carrying his nephew's lifeless body. He had been stabbed in the heart.

When the guards told Don Juan Manuel where the body had been found, a horrific realisation struck him. In the darkness, he had unknowingly murdered the very person he loved most. Overcome with guilt and horror, he finally recognised the evil he had committed.

Seeking redemption, Don Juan Manuel confessed his crimes to a priest, revealing every life he had taken.

The priest, though shocked, gave him one chance to save his soul. As penance, he was ordered to walk alone through the streets at midnight until he reached the Chapel of the Espiración, which faced the Plazuela de Santo Domingo. There, beneath the gallows, he was to kneel and recite the rosary, praying for forgiveness.

Don Juan Manuel welcomed the punishment, relieved that salvation was still within reach.

That night, as he stepped out of his house to begin his penance, whispers filled the air around him. He heard mournful voices, the voices of those he had killed. A small bell began to ring, a chilling, relentless sound, and it filled him with terror. Fear twisted his stomach, and he turned back, unable to go on.

The next morning, he returned to the priest, begging for a different penance, but the priest refused.

"Do as you have been commanded," he warned, "or perish in your sins and burn in Hell forever."

That night, Don Juan Manuel tried again. This time, he made it halfway to the chapel before the voices and the bell overwhelmed him, forcing him to turn back in fear.

Again, he pleaded with the priest for another punishment, but once more, his request was denied.

On his third attempt, he managed to walk three-quarters of the way before his terror overtook him, sending him fleeing once more.

For the final time, Don Juan Manuel approached the priest, desperate and trembling, but the priest remained firm, "There is no other way to save your soul."

That night, knowing this was his last chance at redemption, he forced himself forward, despite the whispers and the terrible ringing of the bell. His stomach twisted in fear, his body trembled, but he pressed on, for he knew his only alternative was eternal damnation.

At last, he reached the Plazuela de Santo Domingo and knelt beneath the gallows in front of the Chapel of the Espiración. There, with shaking hands, he recited the rosary, desperate for forgiveness.

By morning, word had spread, and the entire city, from the Viceroy to the humblest cargadores, rushed to the Plazuela de Santo Domingo., and there, they saw a terrifying sight

Don Juan Manuel was hanging from the gallows, dead.

No human hands had placed him there. It was the work of the angels themselves, delivering divine justice for his sins.

The Silver Omelette

This story has been adapted from a tale originally told by Charles F. Lummis in The Enchanted Burro And Other Stories As I Have Known Them From Maine To Chile And California, published in 1912 by A. C. McClurg & Co., Chicago. The book featured a diverse selection of tales gathered from different regions, spanning from Maine to Chile and California. Each story offered a glimpse into the folklore, myths, and cultural traditions of the places they originate from.

Flipping the mixture within six inches of the ceiling and catching it neatly back in the frying pan, as any skilled frontiersman should, was an impressive feat. But no matter how much you blink in disbelief, the fact remains that we were now sitting down to an omelette two and a half feet thick and an astonishing one hundred and ten feet across! A meal worth more than your entire household could consume in a lifetime.

The real problem, however, was that the chef was away. Don Ygnacio, who had been preparing these gigantic omelettes for thirty years and had the knack for it, was out in Dolores that day. In his place, left in charge of the kitchen, was a nervous eighteen-year-old lad with a fuzzy face, who had never in his life attempted to turn a Guanajuato omelette.

Now, Guanajuato is one of the oldest and richest silver-mining regions in the world. This picturesque Mexican city, founded over three and a half centuries ago, has produced more than a billion dollars in silver bullion and still hasn't exhausted its wealth. Back in 1527, a Spanish miner in Mexico invented the cheapest and simplest method for extracting silver from ore, the patio process. For centuries, this method has been used to process the vast silver deposits of Mexico and Peru. Even today, haciendas dedicated to this process remain some of the most fascinating features of Spanish America's great silver camps.

Each hacienda is like a small fortress, complete with strong ramparts and corner towers, loop-holed for muskets. Inside, there are huge sheds for the primitive ore-grinding process, a comfortable residence for the administrator, workers' quarters, stables for hundreds of mules, and most notably, enormous stone skillets, where the world's largest omelettes are "cooked".

In Spanish America, the word for omelette is torta. Literally, it means "cake", with the "of eggs" part understood. But in the mining world, the term refers to a very different kind of omelette, one made of wet-ground silver ore, mixed with the necessary chemicals to extract the metal. Visually, it looks less like an omelette and more like an enormous mud pie.

At the Hacienda de los Cipreses, one of these "omelettes" was currently in progress. Patient burro caravans had carried loads of broken grey rock down from the legendary Valenciana silver mine, enough to create forty-six heaps, each weighing 3,200 pounds. The ore had then been fed into the massive grinding mill, where a huge, iron-bound wheel, driven by straining mules, slowly crushed the rocks into finer and finer particles until they sifted through a screen into storage bins.

From there, the ground ore was shovelled into wet-grinding arrastras, thirty large stone vats, where mules turned their whims, dragging granite blocks that crushed the gravel into a fine paste. This mud-like mixture was then transferred to a large sedimentation tank, known as the cajete, where the excess water was drained away. Finally, the thickened sludge was spread out onto the stone-paved patio, where it would become a torta.

Now, while almost anyone could grind ore, whether dry or wet, knowing exactly how to process it was a different matter entirely. Testing the mud, determining how much silver it contained per ton, and calculating precisely how much salt and mercury were needed to extract the metal, that was no job for an amateur. When dealing with fifty thousand dollars' worth of silver, accuracy was critical. Extracting that fortune from 150 tons of mud required scientific precision, and there was no room for error.

Yet, despite the risks, Don Ygnacio had no choice but to leave. Taking four of his most trusted men, all armed for protection, he set off, for in those days, brigands lurked along every Mexican highway. The only person available to take charge was his young and inexperienced nephew, Alberto.

Fortunately, before leaving, Don Ygnacio had time to leave precise instructions for the batch currently being processed. "Add this much salt and this much mercury," he advised. "That should do the trick.

But watch it carefully, and if necessary, adjust the mix accordingly. Take care, and best of luck!"

For seventeen days, Alberto had paced anxiously across the stone-paved courtyard and through the vast sheds where the dry mill and wet mill noisily ground their materials for the next torta. Every so often, he would glance, subtly but deliberately, towards the last room on the administrador's porch, where behind a thick wooden door, he had personally stacked forty-pound bars of pure silver, refined from the previous batch.

The washing, concentration, and smelting process had been straightforward enough under his supervision. He had ensured that a significant worth of metal had been safely stored.

As for the current torta, his assays confirmed that Don Ygnacio's initial estimate had been entirely accurate. Still, Alberto hoped the old manager would return in time, not only to determine whether the usual eighteen days of processing had been sufficient, but also to decide on the next batch's composition.

For a young man who had observed the making of a hundred tortas but never been responsible for one, the weight of expectation was immense. The pressure was evident, his once broad shoulders no longer seemed as squared, nor his chest as full, as when he had first taken charge.

In the quarter-acre pit where the torta was both beaten and refined, a dozen men and older boys waded thigh-deep in the thick sludge, driving blindfolded mules through the mess to mix the mercury with the silver ore. The poor beasts had their eyes covered to protect them from the harsh elements, as they trudged endlessly, dragging the heavy boards that stirred the mixture. It was nearly noon. In five minutes, the exhausted mules would finally be relieved from their six-hour shift.

As Alberto walked towards the well-tower, his eyes were drawn to a young worker, a broad-shouldered lad, slouching behind a white mule at the edge of the mud pit. The boy's dull, vacant expression gave him the air of someone who was simply enduring another monotonous day. Yet Alberto knew better. It was one thing to trudge through mud for eighteen cents a day, but another thing entirely to manage mud worth a year's salary per ton.

That was when he heard it.

"S-s-t!"

Alberto froze. It couldn't be. Could it? He turned his head slightly, just enough to confirm what he had already feared. The mud-stained young Indian had actually whispered to him.

"Careful!" the lad murmured, as Alberto approached the stone water trough. His eyes never left his mule, nor did his posture change. He tugged at the tired animal's reins, pretending to scold it, while speaking in hushed tones between his curses.

"Move, you stubborn beast! (Young master, the bandits!)"

"For how long must I teach you to walk? (Some of them are inside the hacienda!)"

"Useless creature! Do you not understand the rein? (They are planning to strike tonight!)"

Then, without a single sideways glance, the boy moved on, shuffling through the thick mud, dragging the mule behind him. Alberto's face turned pale. But he was no fool. He stole a glance at the nearest worker, a newcomer from the countryside. The man was tall and powerfully built, with a deep scar along his cheek, shifty eyes, and a long, curved nose, hence his nickname, Narigudo, "Big Nose."

Narigudo's gaze flickered sharply, first towards the departing Indian, then towards Alberto himself.

Keeping his expression neutral, Alberto turned and walked calmly towards the well-house.

The old silver bell in the belfry clanged. Noon had arrived.

The mud-soaked workers, both human and animal, scrambled out of the pit. In seconds, their harnesses and blindfolds were cast onto the flagstones, and the mules, suddenly energised, went braying and galloping through the main gate, heading towards the highway stream, where they could drink and bathe. This small, unassuming brook had likely carried more silver than any other stream on Earth.

A moment later, a thunderous stampede followed, as one hundred mules from the mills came charging down the stone paths. Though they still had another six-hour shift ahead, they knew the rhythm of the day, and they knew when it was time for a break. They surged forward like a cavalry charge, colliding into each other as they forced their way out through the gates, in a frenzy that should have killed some of them outright.

Alberto had laughed at this chaotic scene a thousand times. But today, his mind was elsewhere. He reached for the bucket by the pump wheel, splashed cold water on his face, and ran a hand through his hair. His mind was racing.

Bandits, tonight. Inside men, already within the hacienda. Nearly fifty thousand dollars in silver, locked in the administrador's room. And he, alone.

Alberto had been raised with care, shielded from danger, and never burdened with true responsibility. Now, for the first time in his life, he was utterly terrified. Yet deep within him, something stirred, a distant, forgotten inheritance from the men who had conquered these wild lands centuries before.

Within five minutes, the young administrador was making his rounds as usual, occasionally stopping to pick up a sample of ore, studying it with great interest. As he passed groups of workers eating their lunch, he couldn't shake the feeling that some eyes were watching him more intently than usual. It sent a chill down his spine, but outwardly, he remained calm, his mind racing as he tried to solve what was, without a doubt, the toughest problem he had ever faced.

Suddenly, a thought struck him, and he turned on his heel, heading straight down to the patio. In full view of the workers, he took careful samples from the mud mixture, examining them critically before carrying them off to the assay room. Ten minutes later, he emerged once more and strode towards the labourers.

"A half-day holiday for everyone," he announced. "The torta looks ready to me, and Don Ygnacio should arrive tonight to confirm it. Go now, but be back at dawn."

The announcement instantly ended lunch. The men sprang to their feet, some calling out, "Many thanks, sir!", already heading towards the gates.

All except Narigudo, "Big Nose", and four others. Unlike their eager comrades, they continued eating slowly, finishing their food rather than discarding it. Instead of rushing off, they exchanged glances, first at each other, then at the men leaving.

"Señor, I do not think it is ready," Narigudo muttered sullenly.

Alberto didn't hesitate. "And who asked for your opinion?" he replied coolly. "Are you responsible for profits and losses here?"

Narigudo fell silent, but his scowl deepened as he reluctantly rose to follow his departing comrades. Alberto watched until they had all left before heading into his office. Five minutes later, he stepped outside again. The hacienda was completely empty.

So far, so good. It seemed there were only five traitors, and for now, they were gone. All he needed to do now was lock the big gate, and then figure out what to do next. Feeling slightly more at ease, Alberto walked over to the large shed, pausing by the trundle-mill as he thought through his options. Should he leave the hacienda secured and ride up to the city to warn the authorities? Then, a sound, barely even a whisper, shattered his thoughts.

Alberto whirled around. The blood drained from his face. Fifteen feet away, standing barefoot in the doorway of the ore shed, was Narigudo with an ugly smirk on his face.

"Young Excellency," he sneered, his tone dripping with mockery, "you've locked me in. Give me the keys, so I can leave."

Alberto found his voice. "In this hacienda," he said steadily, "it is customary to obey the administrador, not to command him. I will let you out when I go to the gate."

Narigudo's smirk twisted into a snarl. "Oh, it's the administrador, is it?" His voice darkened with fury. "Then give me the keys, before I rip you apart!"

Without hesitation, the giant of a man lunged forward. Alberto stumbled back, but his mind was clear. He could not let Narigudo get the key to the bullion room. Never. With a sudden burst of movement, he yanked the heavy keys from his belt and flung them away, just as Narigudo's massive hand clamped onto his shoulder.

With a furious curse, Narigudo threw Alberto against a wooden post, then dived after the keys in desperation. But he was too late. The keys clattered down into the deep drain, just out of reach.

Narigudo let out a roar of frustration. "Just wait!" he bellowed. "I'll get them back, and you'll pay for the trouble!"

He plunged into the drain opening, turning his head just long enough to shoot Alberto a murderous glare. Alberto's heart pounded against his ribs. There was no escape. The gate was locked from the outside, which meant he was trapped in here, too. Narigudo would get the keys, and then what? Then, he would kill him.

Alberto's breath came in sharp gasps, but then a desperate idea flickered in his mind. A large wooden trough stood nearby, tilted on one side. Without hesitation, he shoved his shoulder into it, tipping it forward. From beneath, there was a muffled roar of rage. Narigudo was trapped!

A queer, breathless laugh escaped Alberto. But his relief was short-lived. The trough shook violently beneath him. Narigudo was already fighting back, using his immense strength to lift the wooden weight off himself.

Alberto held his breath. He had underestimated the man's power. If he stepped off for even a moment, Narigudo would break free, and then He would kill him. Panic surged through him, but there was no time to think. He couldn't risk leaving the trough, but he also couldn't stay there forever. The nearest sacks of ore were too far away, and he didn't dare leave his position long enough to fetch them. Trapped in a nightmare of fear, he clung to the trough, trying to make himself heavier, all the while whispering frantic prayers to every saint he could name.

Suddenly, he let out a wild shout. The whim! There stood the great vertical wheel, with its long wooden pole reaching out just two feet off the ground, and it was only about ten feet away.

Alberto sprang into action, his feet pounding noisily on the wooden trough. He leapt down, then back up again, dashing forward before charging back onto the trough. Now, his mind was as clear as a bell. In one swift movement, he grabbed the heavy pole and yanked it with all his strength. The old mill creaked and shifted an inch. He jumped back onto the trough, then back to the pole for another mighty tug. Again, and again, a dozen times over, he repeated the action. With each effort, the reluctant wheel groaned forward, inch by inch, until finally, the end of the pole just overlapped the edge of the trough.

All was silent below. The prisoner, confused by the chaotic noises overhead, waited, trying to make sense of what was happening. Just as he began to struggle again, Alberto, his body braced against the trough, slowly, but surely, dragged the pole further in. With one final, fierce pull, his task was done. The massive horizontal pole now hung directly over the centre of the trough.

Exhausted, Alberto leaned against the wheel, his breath ragged. A weak smile crossed his lips as the trough suddenly jerked upwards, just three inches. Then, with a heavy thump, it slammed into the pole and dropped back down with a bang. The trap was locked. Alberto didn't stop until he collapsed, breathless, on the steps of the office.

Dusk was falling and there was no time to lose. There were plenty of muskets stored in the armoury, but Narigudo had the key. Fortunately, one gun remained in the office. With shaking hands,

Alberto loaded it, then climbed into the turret above the gate, crouching in the darkness, waiting. Then, an idea struck him. He chuckled to himself, dashed down the courtyard, and disappeared into the stables.

Twenty minutes later, he returned to the tower. The stables were empty. The office drawer, the one Don Ygnacio used to store fireworks for festival nights, was also completely cleared out.

Meanwhile, a hundred drowsy mules were now huddled together at the entrance, a thick rope stretched behind them, blocking their retreat. Behind the rope, a neat line of small red firecrackers lay scattered across the ground.

At nine o'clock, a faint tap came at the gate. "Narigudo!" someone whispered. A moment later, louder and more impatiently, "Narigudo! Are you asleep? Open up!"

Alberto almost laughed. He squared his shoulders and called out sharply, "Not a shot until I give the order! As for you fools, look at the gate! And as for your Narigudo, he's well out of the way!"

A scramble of movement followed. Clearly, the bandits had pulled back, confused by the unexpected turn of events. For half an hour, a tense silence followed, but then there was a sudden charge! With a thunderous crash, something slammed against the gate.

"Not yet!" shouted Alberto. "Wait for my command!"

But the bandits weren't fooled. If there were real defenders, they would have fired by now. Again, the battering ram smashed into the gate, making the wood tremble under the impact.

Alberto's finger twitched on the trigger. Should he fire? If he missed, they could break through before he reloaded. And then? Thinking fast, he propped the musket against the wall, then crept down into the courtyard. There was another crash and the gate shuddered violently. It was starting to give way.

The next blow was devastating, and one of the gate's leaves began to creak, the kind of deep, splintering groan that always precedes collapse.

Then there was a sudden flash in the courtyard. A sharp s-s-sizz-sizz! Pop! Bang! Bang! B-b-b-bang! The firecrackers exploded in rapid succession. The gate reeled, then fell outward with a crash.

And with the roar of an avalanche, the terrified mules stampeded through the gap. A chaotic blur of hooves and bodies slammed into the cluster of bandits, trampling and scattering them as if they were leaves in the wind.

From far up the cobbled highway, a loud battle cry rang out, followed by pistol shots and the thunder of galloping hooves. Two minutes later, Don Ygnacio and his men charged into the courtyard, where a collapsed young hero lay, breathless, beside a pile of spent firecrackers.

Legend Of The Obedient Dead Nun

This story has been adapted from a tale originally told by Thomas A. Janvier in Legends Of The City Of Mexico, published in 1910 by Harper & Brothers Publishers, New York. Legends of the City of Mexico delves into the rich cultural heritage of Mexico, exploring the myths and legends that have been passed down through generations. The book included a diverse range of stories, drawing from Aztec, Spanish, and indigenous Mexican traditions.

It was only after she had died, Señor, that this nun obeyed the Mother Superior's command, and that is why it was considered a miracle. It also proved her virtue and holiness, though, to be fair, there was no need for proof, for everyone already knew of her goodness before she passed away.

My grandmother told me that this event took place in the Convent of Santa Brígida when her own mother was a little girl, so, as you can imagine, Señor, this was not something that happened yesterday. In those days, the convent was thriving. It was large, full of nuns, and had more wealth than it needed, allowing for great acts of charity. But, as you know, Señor, today the convent no longer exists, and only the church remains. It was in that very church that the miracle occurred, and in its choir lies the coffin of Sor Teresa, the very same coffin that was too small for her. So, as you can see, this story must be true.

The nun in question, before taking her vows, was Señorita Teresa Ysabel de Villavicencio, the daughter of a wealthy landowner from Veracruz. She was very tall, and it was this great height that caused the problem, and she was also very beautiful.

She entered the Convent of Santa Brígida and took her religious vows after suffering a broken heart. The man who deceived her was Señor Carraza, the Librarian to the Royal and Pontifical University, a position that should have meant he was a respectable man. What he did to wrong her, Señor, I do not know, but whatever it was, it drove Sor Teresa into the convent in haste.

Once there, she was so devout, so humble, and so obedient that the Mother Superior held her up as an example to the other nuns. No matter what she was told to do, she did it, and never once did she question or complain.

One day, as the convent busily prepared for the great festival of Nuestra Señora de Guadalupe, Sor Teresa made a sudden and shocking declaration. She announced that, although she was helping with preparations, she would not live to see the festival. She knew her time had come, and her final hours on Earth were drawing near.

And so it was.

A short while later, lying on her hard wooden bed, wearing beneath her habit the wire shirt of a penitent, and surrounded by her grieving sisters, Sor Teresa passed away, just as she had predicted.

And what illness took her, you ask? None at all. She simply died, as if her soul had chosen to leave.

Because of the upcoming festival, Sor Teresa had to be buried that very night. The nuns prepared her grave and sent for a coffin. And this, Señor, is when the trouble began. Perhaps the carpenter misjudged her measurements, or perhaps, in the flurry of preparations, the nuns had given the wrong size. Either way, when the coffin arrived, Sor Teresa did not fit inside. Her long legs stuck out past the end of the casket, and with nightfall fast approaching, there was no time to build another one. The nuns stood helpless, staring at Sor Teresa's holy feet, which refused to fit neatly inside the coffin.

With the festival the next day, the urgency of the situation grew, but no one could think of a solution. Then, one of the older nuns, known for her wisdom, whispered to the Mother Superior, "Sor Teresa was the most obedient among us in life, surely, even in death, she will obey a direct order?"

She suggested that the Mother Superior command Sor Teresa to fit into her coffin, for if she obeyed, the problem would be solved. And if she did not, well, no harm would be done, and they could try something else. Seeing no other choice, the Mother Superior agreed.

The entire convent gathered around, the candle of Nuestro Amo was lit, and, in a solemn voice, the Mother Superior gave her command, "Daughter, as in life you were a model of humility and obedience, I now order and command you, by your vow of obedience, to adjust yourself within your coffin, so that we may bury you and you may rest in peace."

And then, Señor, before everyone's eyes, the miracle occurred. Sor Teresa's body began to shrink. Slowly, her feet drew back, first, until they were just at the edge of the coffin, then just over the edge, and finally, with a small but holy thud, her feet landed neatly inside the coffin's base. She had obeyed. She now fit perfectly.

With great reverence and awe, the nuns buried her in the convent's choir, where she rests to this day. So you see, Señor, this story must be true, for her bones still lie buried in the very coffin that was too small for her.

The Three Hunters

This story is my own adaptation of a traditional regional tale. This version of the tale was largely informed by sources from Nicaragua.

In the deep heart of Central America, where the jungle grew ancient and untamed, three hunters made their home. They were Rico, Miguel, and Carlos, men shaped by the wilderness, their bodies lean from the hunt, their eyes sharp as hawks. They moved as the jungle did, their spirits tied to its rhythms, in tune with the whisper of the wind through the canopy, the rustle of unseen creatures, and the distant calls of birds that knew secrets older than man.

Of the three, Rico was the eldest. He carried deep wisdom in his gaze, his hands calloused from years of toil and quiet reverence. Miguel and Carlos, younger and bolder, still carried the recklessness of youth, the kind that dares without knowing the cost.

One humid morning, when the mist still clung to the trees and the ground steamed with the rising sun, the three men set out on a hunt like any other. Armed with bows, spears, and old flintlocks, they ventured deeper than they ever had before, lured by the promise of untouched land where the prey grew fatter and slower, unspoiled by human presence. They did not know then that the jungle had led them astray on purpose.

By midday, the hunters found themselves in a place unknown, where the trees parted like supplicants, and a great clearing yawned before them, silent and unnatural in its stillness. At its centre stood a tree, unlike any they had seen before. Its trunk was colossal, its bark an iridescent gold that shimmered under the fractured sunlight. Its roots twisted through the earth like veins, pulsing faintly, as if they were alive with breath. Above, its branches stretched like a titan's fingers, reaching for the sky, yet refusing to touch it.

Beneath it, a pool of water gleamed like a polished mirror, impossibly clear. Silver fish glided just below the surface, but their movements were wrong, too smooth, too silent, as if they swam in something thicker than water. A chill settled on Rico's skin, despite the heat of the jungle. His instincts, those sharpened by a lifetime in the wild, screamed at him to turn back.

"This place is not ours," he murmured.

But Miguel laughed, his voice ringing too loudly in the eerie quiet. "Look at it, Rico! This tree, this place, there must be something here. Something valuable."

Carlos smirked, kneeling at the edge of the pool, letting his fingers trail through the water. "You see ghosts everywhere, old man. Maybe the jungle has finally rattled your mind."

Rico tensed, his gut twisting. The moment Carlos's fingers broke the surface of the water, the entire clearing exhaled. A mist rose from the pool like living breath, thick and white, curling around them like a living creature. The air physically shuddered. Then came the sound, a groaning, deep and ancient, as if the jungle itself was moaning in pain. And suddenly, the world fell apart.

Miguel and Carlos screamed. The mist swallowed them whole, wrapping around their limbs like tendrils of living smoke. They staggered, their bodies twisting in ways unnatural, their lungs filled with air too thick to breathe.

Rico, standing at the tree's roots, could not reach them. His body refused to move, pinned by a force older than the sun, something that pressed against him with the weight of thousands of years.

And then, from the depths of the mist, it appeared. A figure, towering and inhuman, stepped forward. It wore robes spun from gold and earth, woven with vines and the filigree of leaves, yet its skin was the colour of stone, its eyes deep as the abyss. It was the Spirit of the Earth, the Guardian of the Sacred Tree.

Its voice rumbled through the ground, each word making the soil tremble beneath Rico's feet. "You have trespassed."

Rico's heart thundered in his chest, but he forced himself to meet the Spirit's gaze. "We did not know," he said, his voice steady despite the terror in his bones.

The Spirit tilted its head, its expression unreadable. "You knew enough to fear. And yet you let them stay."

Miguel and Carlos gasped, their bodies wracked with pain as the mist tightened around them.

"The land remembers," the Spirit said, its voice hollow and terrible. "It remembers the blood spilled upon it. The lives stolen. The balance broken."

Rico saw, flashing before his eyes, visions of the past, of men before them, hunters, invaders, all those who had taken more than they had given. He saw their bones swallowed by the roots, their bodies fed to the tree, their voices now part of the wailing wind that haunted the jungle at night.

The Spirit lifted a hand of stone and soil, and the mist around Miguel and Carlos vibrated. "What shall be your payment?"

Rico did not hesitate.

"Take me," he said. "Let them go."

The Spirit studied him, the silence stretching too long. Then, at last, it lowered its hand. "A rare thing," it murmured. "To find a man who understands the lore of the land."

The mist vanished. Miguel and Carlos collapsed to the ground, gasping for air. Their bodies were untouched, but their eyes…their eyes held something forever broken.

Rico turned to them, his voice firm. "Go. Now."

Miguel clawed at the dirt, his eyes wide with horror. "Rico…no! We can't…"

"GO.!

A great wind howled through the clearing, and the jungle obeyed. The roots shifted, the trees closed in, sealing the way shut behind them.

Miguel and Carlos ran.

Rico stayed.

Miguel and Carlos never spoke of what had happened. They never spoke of Rico, nor of the forbidden clearing, nor of the towering tree that now haunted their dreams. Yet, when the wind howled through the jungle, when the branches creaked like bones beneath the weight of the sky, they swore they could hear a voice within it, low, steady, eternal. A voice just like Rico's.

And somewhere, in the deepest part of the jungle, where the earth never forgets, a tree grew taller than any other, its roots wrapped around something sacred, and beneath its branches, the forest whispers to this day Rico's name.

Legend Of The Puente Del Clérigo

This story has been adapted from a tale originally told by Thomas A. Janvier in Legends Of The City Of Mexico, published in 1910 by Harper & Brothers Publishers, New York. Legends of the City of Mexico delves into the rich cultural heritage of Mexico, exploring the myths and legends that have been passed down through generations. The book included a diverse range of stories, drawing from Aztec, Spanish, and indigenous Mexican traditions.

The priest who was murdered and thrown from the bridge, Señor, was a good and honourable man, and there was little justification for his killing. He came from a respected family, as did the gentleman who killed him and the young lady caught up in it all. Because of this, and because murdering a priest is sacrilege, the crime caused a great scandal throughout the town.

This happened several hundred years ago, Señor, at a time when a beautiful young woman named Doña Margarita Jáuregui lived on what is now called Puente del Clérigo (The Cleric's Bridge Street). Being an orphan, she lived with her uncle, Padre Don Juan de Nava, a man of high standing who was a knight of the Orders of Santiago and Calatrava.

In those days, the street had few houses because it formed a causeway between the City and the Indian town of Tlaltelolco. For protection, a wide ditch separated the Spanish settlement from the Indian town, with a bridge connecting them. Over time, Tlaltelolco was absorbed into the City, and both the ditch and the bridge disappeared.

At the Viceroy's court, there lived a wealthy and titled Portuguese nobleman named Don Duarte de Sarraza. The Viceroy, Conde de Salvatierra, held him in high esteem, believing him to be a loyal and good-hearted man.

Don Duarte fell deeply in love with Doña Margarita, and she loved him in return. However, her uncle, Padre Don Juan, knew that Don Duarte was not the man he appeared to be. He was a gambler and a man of vice, unfit for his niece. Padre Don Juan forbade their courtship, and Don Duarte was furious.

One night, Don Duarte stood outside Doña Margarita's window, whispering his love through the iron grating. As he did so, he spotted Padre Don Juan walking home along the causeway, illuminated only by the stars. Seized by hatred and rage, Don Duarte hurried to the bridge and waited in the darkness.

When Padre Don Juan reached the crossing, Don Duarte leapt out and stabbed him in the head with his dagger. The blade sank deep into the priest's skull, and Don Duarte could not pull it free. So, rather than waste time, he shoved the body over the bridge, letting it fall into the water below, the dagger still lodged firmly in place. Then he vanished into the night, leaving no trace of his crime.

To avoid suspicion, Don Duarte stayed away from Doña Margarita for nearly a year. But his love for her was too strong, and at last, he could bear it no longer. Late one night, he returned to her window, intending to persuade her to elope so he could take her away forever.

But what actually happened that night remains a mystery. What we do know is this:

At dawn, the neighbours discovered Don Duarte's lifeless body lying on the Bridge of the Cleric. Strangling him, a bony knee pressed into his chest, with two skeletal hands wrapped around his throat, was a skeleton. It was dressed in a black cassock, the robe of a priest. And in its skull, still nailed fast, was a rusty dagger.

From that moment on, everyone knew the truth. It was Don Duarte who had murdered Padre Don Juan. And it was Padre Don Juan's own vengeful spirit that had risen from the grave to kill Don Duarte in just revenge.

The Man Who Sold His Soul

This story is my own adaptation of a traditional regional tale. This version of the tale was largely informed by sources from Nicaragua.

There was a man named Alejandro de León, and he was a man cursed by his own hunger. Not the hunger of the stomach, nor even the hunger of the flesh, his hunger was more insidious. He craved gold, power, and influence, and he would devour all in his path to have them.

He had bought and sold everything a man could, land, slaves, secrets, even blood, and yet his hunger never waned. He climbed the social ladder by stepping on the corpses of the desperate, and he built his empire with bricks of broken promises. Yet even with chests of gold, servants at his feet, and the most beautiful women draped over his arm, Alejandro was not satisfied.

And so, when the Stranger came, his arrival felt almost... inevitable.

It was on a humid evening in the heart of Nicaraguan City, beneath a sky blackened by storm clouds, that Alejandro saw him. The marketplace was alive. Merchants hawked their wares, beggars whispered their pleas, and the smell of roasted meat and damp earth mingled in the air. But even amidst the chaotic symphony of life, Alejandro noticed the Stranger immediately. He was impossibly still, standing at the crossroads where the shadows of the old cathedral swallowed the lantern light. His cloak was the black of midnight, and his eyes burned silver, like coins reflecting the moon. His very presence seemed to bend the world around him, making him more real than anything else.

Alejandro, ever the man of transactions, felt an irresistible pull. "Who are you?" he asked, stepping closer.

The Stranger did not blink. He did not move. And yet, his whispering voice filled the space between them, as though it had slithered straight into Alejandro's ear. "I am a dealer of souls, Don Alejandro. And I have come to offer you a bargain."

Alejandro's pulse quickened. He had made many deals, some cruel, some clever, but never had he encountered a merchant of souls. "What kind of bargain?" he asked, his greed already coiling around his heart like a serpent.

The Stranger lifted a small glass vial. It pulsed with a liquid that was not one colour, but all colours, shifting and shimmering like molten opal. "Drink this," the Stranger said, his voice laced with amusement. "And you shall have all the riches your heart desires. The world will bend to your will, and even kings shall envy you."

Alejandro's fingers itched to take it, but something in his rotting conscience stirred. "And what do you get in return?"

The Stranger's smile widened. His teeth were too white, too sharp, too many. "Why, only what is already mine, Don Alejandro. Your soul."

Alejandro hesitated. Some forgotten fragment of childhood prayers whispered in the back of his mind, warning him. But he had always laughed at warnings. He took the vial and drank. The moment the liquid touched his tongue, the world screamed in his ears.

It began slowly. At first, he felt warmth, then euphoria, then pure, undiluted power coursing through his veins. His skin hummed, his bones shook with excitement and anticipation. It was as if the universe had bowed before him, surrendering all its treasures. He blinked, and gold spilled from his hands like sand. He exhaled, and jewels rained from the sky. He laughed, and kingdoms trembled.

For weeks, Alejandro drowned himself in wealth. He purchased entire towns, adorned himself with chains of ruby and sapphire, and bathed in basins of melted silver. He hosted feasts where guests ate meat from golden bones, and he commanded the most beautiful women in the land to sit at his feet. He had everything. And yet…he had nothing, because his hunger was still there. He could no longer taste the food, nor could he feel warmth. When he laughed, the room fell silent, as if the sound did not belong to the world anymore. His reflection no longer looked like him, and when he touched his own chest, he felt no heartbeat.

His riches became ash in his hands. His women became shadows that slithered away when he tried to touch them. His home became a tomb, where he sat upon a throne of his own making, surrounded by wealth he could no longer enjoy. And the hunger grew worse.

He tried eating, but it was like chewing on dust. He tried drinking, but the wine was thin and bitter. And when he looked into the mirror, his face was fading, but it was not age that withered him, it was absence. He had sold his soul. And now, there was nothing left of Alejandro de León.

Desperate, he searched for the Stranger, but the man was nowhere. He scoured the alleys of the City, visited the witches in the hills, begged the priests in the cathedrals. None could help him.

"You made a deal, Alejandro," one old bruja whispered. "And the Dealer always collects."

And still, he searched. He searched until his wealth was spent. He searched until his hands were bloodied from digging through the dirt, looking for a way back. He searched until his name was forgotten. Until he was forgotten.

They say that if you walk the cobblestone streets at night, when the lanterns flicker and the wind whispers in tongues long dead, you may see a shadow of a man, a man whose clothes, once fine, are now tattered and ruined. You may see a man whose fingers twitch as if searching for gold that is no longer there, a man who wanders endlessly, his eyes hollow, his voice thin. He searches, still, for the Stranger, for his soul, and for the taste of life he can never have again.

They say if you listen closely, you can hear his voice, echoing from the alleyways, in a whisper softer than the wind, saying, "Have you seen him? The man in black? I need to find him. I need to…please…just one more deal."

But no one ever answers, because the Stranger always collects.

Legend Of The Mulata De Córdoba

This story has been adapted from a tale originally told by Thomas A. Janvier in Legends Of The City Of Mexico, published in 1910 by Harper & Brothers Publishers, New York. Legends of the City of Mexico delves into the rich cultural heritage of Mexico, exploring the myths and legends that have been passed down through generations. The book included a diverse range of stories, drawing from Aztec, Spanish, and indigenous Mexican traditions.

It is well known that the Mulata of Córdoba, a woman of extraordinary beauty, was believed to be in league with the devil.

She lived in Córdoba, the town near Veracruz, famous for its coffee plantations and delicious mangoes. She had been around for so long that even the oldest living person today was not yet born when she first appeared. No one knew who her parents were, nor where she had come from. And so, she was simply called La Mulata de Córdoba, nothing more.

One of her greatest mysteries was that, despite the passage of time, she never seemed to age.

She led what appeared to be a good and virtuous life, always helping those in need, feeding the hungry, and dressing modestly, with an air of grace and cleanliness. Yet, at the same time, she was rumoured to be a powerful witch. People claimed to have seen her in two places at once, one moment in Córdoba, the next in the City, and even elsewhere, all at precisely the same time. Others swore they had seen her flying above rooftops, her black eyes flashing sparks as she soared through the night sky.

Even more unsettling were the stories that the devil visited her every night. Her neighbours insisted that through the cracks of her tightly shut doors and windows, an unnatural light would shine, as if the entire house were aflame.

Yet, despite these whispers, she attended Mass regularly and received the Sacrament at the proper times.

She looked down on everyone, and because of this cold arrogance, many believed that the true master of her beauty was none other than the Prince of Darkness himself. It seemed to make sense, for every young man in town was utterly bewitched by her, following her like moths to a flame.

People told extraordinary tales of her supernatural powers, claiming that she was as miraculous as Santa Rita de Cascia, the Patron Saint of Impossible Causes. Unmarried women sought her help in finding husbands. Impoverished noblewomen begged her for jewels and fine gowns so they could be presented at the Viceroy's court. Miners prayed for her blessing so they might strike silver. Ageing soldiers, cast aside and forgotten, turned to her for new commissions.

Such was her reputation that even today, when someone requests the impossible, the response is often, "I am not the Mulata of Córdoba!"

One day, the Mulata of Córdoba was seized and brought to the City, thrown into the prison of the Holy Office, the Inquisition. The news shook the city to its core. Some claimed that a rejected lover, furious at her scorn, had denounced her to the Inquisition. Others whispered that the Holy Office was not so much interested in her witchcraft as in her enormous wealth, for it was said that when she was arrested, ten barrels filled with gold dust were confiscated alongside her. For days, the entire city could speak of nothing else.

Many years passed, and the rumours surrounding the witch of Córdoba were nearly forgotten. Then, one morning, the city was shocked by startling news. No one knew exactly where it had come from, but it spread like wildfire.

At the next auto-da-fé, the witch of Córdoba was to walk alongside the unredeemed, carrying the flameless green candle and wearing the tall, conical bonnet of the condemned. She was to be burned at the stake by the Holy Office, in front of the Church of San Diego, at the western edge of what is now the Alameda. Her sins would be cleansed by fire.

But before the city's shock had even subsided, another revelation sent even greater waves through the streets. The witch had escaped! Right before the eyes of her jailers, she had vanished from the Inquisition's prison, leaving no trace.

Rumours spread wildly. Some whispered, crossing themselves, that the devil himself had come to her aid. Others speculated that, despite their sacred duty, even Inquisitors were only human, and that perhaps her beauty had secured her freedom. Theories and speculation ran rampant, but in truth, no one ever knew what had really happened.

This is what really happened...

One day, the Chief Inquisitor visited the witch's cell, hoping to reason with her, to bring her to repentance. She had not been placed in one of the cramped, foul dungeons typical of the Inquisition. Instead, she had been given a large, high-ceilinged chamber, as if the authorities sensed that she was no ordinary prisoner.

The Inquisitor stepped into the cell and froze in amazement. Before him, covering the entire wall, was a massive charcoal drawing of a great ship, meticulously detailed. Every mast, every sail, every rope had been rendered with perfect accuracy. As he stood staring in disbelief, the witch turned towards him, her black eyes glittering with mischief.

She spoke in a mocking tone, "Tell me, Holy Father, what does this ship lack to make it perfect?"

The Inquisitor frowned, then replied sternly, "Unhappy woman! It is you who are lacking, lacking repentance, lacking salvation! As for this ship, it is perfect in every way… it needs only to sail."

A wicked smile spread across the witch's lips. "Then sail it shall… and very far indeed!"

Her words sent a shiver down the Inquisitor's spine. "Impossible!" he exclaimed, his eyes darting between her and the ship.

Still smiling, she replied, "Watch and see."

With that, she leapt into the air and landed on the ship's deck, as though it were real and solid. She took hold of the tiller, standing at the stern, her expression filled with dark amusement.

Then, a miracle, or a curse, unfolded before his eyes. The ship's sails suddenly filled and billowed out, as if caught by a powerful wind. Slowly, it began to move, at first, creeping forward along the prison wall, then picking up speed. The Inquisitor could do nothing but watch in horror as the ship, with the witch still laughing at the helm, sailed towards the solid stone wall at the end of the chamber. And then it passed straight through the wall. The ship and the witch vanished into the stone, as though the wall had been nothing but air.

For a moment, there was silence. Then, as the last echo of her wicked laughter faded into the distance, the wall closed itself, whole and solid once more.

She was gone.

The Inquisitor, having witnessed the impossible, lost his mind that very moment. His sanity shattered, he was taken away and locked in a madhouse, where he raved incessantly about a beautiful woman in a great ship that had sailed through stone walls and across solid ground. He never recovered. Only death brought him peace.

As for the witch, she was never seen again. But it was widely believed that her master, the devil, had finally claimed her for his own.

And if you doubt it, you need only visit the Escuela de Medicina, which, in those days, was the very building that housed the Inquisition's prison. It still stands to this day, a silent witness to the sorcery that once unfolded within its walls.

confronted them. Hidden in the foliage, the hero-gods wounded Vukub-Cakix, causing him to fall and injure his jaw. In retaliation, he tore off Hun-Ahpu's arm and tortured him, before succumbing to his own injuries.

To retrieve Hun-Ahpu's arm, Hun-Ahpu and Xbalanque sought the help of Xpiyacoc and Xmucane, disguised as sorcerers. They convinced Vukub-Cakix to undergo surgery, replacing his precious teeth with maize grains. Eventually, his death, along with that of his wife Chimalmat, followed.

The hero-gods then dealt with Vukub-Cakix's sons. Zipacna was tricked into a deadly trap by four hundred youths, while Cabrakan was subdued with poisoned food and buried alive. Thus, the family of boastful beings met their end at the hands of the hero-gods.

Feathered Serpent And The Five Suns

This story is my own adaptation of a traditional regional tale. This version of the tale was largely informed by sources from Nicaragua.

Long before the world as we know it existed, there was a time of darkness and chaos. In the heart of Mesoamerica, where the sun kisses the earth and the rainforests teem with life, the gods gathered to create a new world.

Among these divine beings was Quetzalcoatl, the Feathered Serpent, known for his wisdom and benevolence. Quetzalcoatl looked upon the void and saw the potential for creation. With the help of his fellow gods, he set out to bring order to the chaos and give birth to a new era.

The gods laboured tirelessly, shaping the earth and the heavens, until they created the first humans from maize dough. These humans were named after the days of the Aztec calendar – Nahui-Ollin, the first sun, Tlil-Ollin, the second sun, Quiahuitl, the third sun, Atl, the fourth sun, and Ehecatl, the fifth sun.

But the gods knew that the world they had created was fragile, and they feared that it would be consumed by darkness once more. So they devised a plan to prevent this catastrophe from befalling them.

Quetzalcoatl and his brother Tezcatlipoca, the Smoking Mirror, embarked on a journey to the underworld, where they confronted the god of death, Mictlantecuhtli. Through cunning and bravery, they defeated Mictlantecuhtli and retrieved the bones of the previous worlds.

Returning to the surface, Quetzalcoatl and Tezcatlipoca sacrificed themselves to the fire, using their own blood to breathe life into the bones of the fallen gods. From these bones, they created the sun and the moon, ensuring that light would always prevail over darkness.

And so, the five suns shone brightly in the sky, bringing warmth and life to the world. But the gods knew that this peace would not last forever, and that one day, the suns would grow dim and the world would be plunged once again into darkness.

But until that day came, the people of Mesoamerica lived in harmony with the earth, honouring the gods and tending to the sacred flame that burned at the heart of their civilization. And though the Feathered Serpent and his fellow gods had long since departed, their legacy lived on in the hearts and minds of the people, ensuring that the light would never be extinguished.

Legend Of The Altar Del Perdon

This story has been adapted from a tale originally told by Thomas A. Janvier in Legends Of The City Of Mexico, published in 1910 by Harper & Brothers Publishers, New York. Legends of the City of Mexico delves into the rich cultural heritage of Mexico, exploring the myths and legends that have been passed down through generations. The book included a diverse range of stories, drawing from Aztec, Spanish, and indigenous Mexican traditions.

A painter, who by a miracle created the most beautiful depiction of Our Lady of Mercy, the very painting that now adorns the Altar del Perdón in the Cathedral, was, at the start of his life, a terrible sinner. He was a Fleming, and many other things that, in the eyes of his time, placed him firmly on the path to eternal damnation. His sins were so numerous that even Purgatory's torments would have been too lenient, and he was seen as destined for the hottest fires of Hell, crafted by the devil himself.

Yet, despite his wickedness, Don Simón Peyrens was a charming and charismatic young man. He was witty, engaging, and delightful in conversation, which made him a favourite of the Viceroy, who frequently invited him to banquets and festivals at the palace. His patron was Don Gastón de Peralta, Marqués de Falces, the third Viceroy of New Spain, who had arrived in Mexico following the death of Don Luis de Velasco, a man so good that when he ceased to be Viceroy, he was said to have become an angel in the year 1564.

A few years later, during the rule of Don Martín Enríquez de Almanza, the fourth Viceroy, a grand artistic competition was announced by the Cathedral Chapter. Their goal was to beautify the Altar del Perdón, and they offered a prize to the artist who could create the most magnificent painting of Our Lady of Mercy. The winning piece would be placed at the heart of the altar, its crowning glory.

Every painter in Mexico eagerly entered the competition, except Peyrens.

At a banquet in the palace, a nobleman asked him why he, the most talented artist in the colony, had not participated. His answer, delivered with contempt and arrogance, shocked all who heard it, "Painting so-called sacred images is nothing but foolishness and vanity. No amount of gold in the world could tempt me to waste my talents on such nonsense!"

His words scalded the ears of the devout men in attendance. Within moments, news of his blasphemous declaration reached the Archbishop of Mexico, Fray Alonso de Montúfar. In no time at all, Peyrens found himself behind iron bars, imprisoned by the Holy Inquisition, that fearsome enforcer of faith, whose tireless work in rooting out heresy ensured the spiritual purity of the land.

Despite threats, pleadings, and interrogations, Peyrens remained defiant. He refused to renounce his blasphemy, and when offered his freedom in exchange for painting an image of Our Lady, he outright refused. His defiance went so far that when the Familiars of the Inquisition brought him a canvas, brushes, and paint, he tore the canvas to shreds before their eyes.

Days turned into weeks, and weeks into months, yet Peyrens did not waver. The Archbishop, a man of great patience and piety, began to lose his temper, while the Inquisitors lost theirs entirely. In the end, the Holy Office debated the only solution left, to purge his wickedness with heavenly fire.

As it happened, an opportunity for redemption was soon to present itself, whether he sought it or not. At that time, preparations were underway for the very first auto de fé ever held in Mexico. The entire city was in a state of eager anticipation, awaiting the event with great excitement.

The painter, Peyrens, known for his stubborn defiance, was expected to be publicly humiliated. He would be dressed in a yellow robe adorned with a red cross, marking him as a heretic, and would walk among the condemned. The crowd eagerly anticipated watching him burn on the pyre, his sins reduced to ashes, which would then be scattered beyond the city's borders, forever tainting the marshland.

However, none of this came to pass.

By divine intervention, Our Lady of Mercy herself took pity on him. And, in a miracle of her own making, she ensured that everything would unfold quite differently.

One night, as Peyrens lay asleep in his cell within the Inquisition, he suddenly awoke, though he could not tell why. A sweet, unfamiliar fragrance filled the air, so exquisite that, for a moment, he thought he must still be dreaming. It was the very scent of heaven itself, a perfume unknown to mortal senses.

As he lay there, bewildered, a soft, shimmering glow emerged in the darkness. The light grew brighter and brighter, until it surpassed even the sun. And then, within that radiant brilliance, appeared Our Lady of Mercy herself. She shone with such divine splendour that, had it not been for the gentle kindness in her gaze, Peyrens might have perished on the spot, overwhelmed by her presence.

In a voice sweeter than any earthly music, she spoke. "My child, why do you not love me?"

Her words pierced his heart, melting away the pride and bitterness that had hardened it for so long. Overcome with awe and devotion, Peyrens rose from his pallet, knelt before her, and cried out with deep sincerity, "Queen of Heaven, I honour and love you with all my heart and all my soul!"

For a time, he was overcome by a profound peace, as if caught in a dream-like state of joy. And when he came back to himself, the radiant vision had vanished. Yet the heavenly light still lingered, illuminating his cell, and the sweet fragrance of lilies and spikenard remained in the air.

As he pondered this divine mystery, still lost in wonder, he heard the same celestial voice, now distant yet clear as a bell, say, "Now, my child, paint my image!"

Perhaps, in her heavenly haste, Our Lady had forgotten that Peyrens had no canvas, having destroyed it in his fury. Or perhaps, she meant for him to find his own way. Either way, his mind immediately leapt to the solution. Inspired by his vision and trembling with excitement, he turned to the wooden door of his cell. By the light of heaven, breathing in the scent of paradise, he began to paint.

All through the night, he worked, as if in a dream, bringing to life the vision he had seen. Every stroke of his brush captured her divine radiance, and by the time dawn broke, his masterpiece was complete. There, on the oaken door, was the most beautiful depiction of Our Lady ever created. It was a portrait like no other, for it was the only one ever painted by a man who had seen her with mortal eyes.

As is often the case with miracles, this one was met with great reverence. The Archbishop and the Cathedral Chapter, summoned in haste, were so overcome with awe at the miraculous image that they immediately fell to their knees in worship. And once they had finished adoring it, they declared that Peyrens had earned both his freedom and his reward.

The painter was released, showered with riches and honours, and formally absolved of his heresy and sins. The wooden door, now a sacred object, was removed from its hinges, placed within a magnificent silver frame, and enshrined on the Altar del Perdon, where it became its greatest glory.

As for Peyrens himself, I do not know what became of him after that. But of one thing there can be no doubt, the miraculous image still stands on the Altar del Perdon to this day, proof of the divine mercy that saved him.

The Courage of the Little Hummingbird

This story is my own adaptation of a traditional regional tale. This tale is based on Ecuadorian sources.

Deep within the great forests of the Andes Mountains, where the trees kissed the sky and the rivers roared like ancient spirits, there lived a tiny hummingbird named Tini. His feathers shimmered like gemstones, with iridescent hues of emerald, sapphire, and gold. When he flitted between the scarlet heliconias and golden trumpet vines, he seemed less like a bird and more like a streak of light, a living spark in a world of green.

The creatures of the forest adored Tini. Not just for his beauty, but for his unyielding spirit. While most hummingbirds concerned themselves only with nectar and speed, Tini sought adventure. He soared higher, dived faster, and dared to explore the untouched corners of the jungle, where even jaguars feared to tread.

But Tini was about to face a challenge unlike any before, one that would test the very limits of his courage.

One golden morning, as Tini hovered above a crystal-clear stream, dipping his beak into the cool water, a shadow passed over the land. He looked up. The sky, once bright and blue, had begun to darken with thick, curling smoke. A sinister cloud rose from the depths of the jungle, and the air carried a scent of destruction, the acrid stench of fire.

Then came the sounds. Shrieks. Cries. The thunder of fleeing hooves. Tini darted upward, his heart hammering in his tiny chest. Below, the jungle had descended into chaos. Birds screamed warnings as they fled. Monkeys raced through the canopy, their eyes wild with terror. Deer and tapirs charged through the undergrowth, their hooves tearing up the earth. And then Tini saw it. The inferno.

A wall of flames devoured the trees, climbing like a monstrous beast with endless hunger. The fire roared, snapping and crackling as it swallowed everything in its path. The great jungle, Tini's home, was burning.

For the first time in his life, he felt small. Smaller than ever before. A whisper of doubt crept into his mind. I'm just a hummingbird. What can I do? But deep in his heart, something stronger than fear took root. I must try, he thought.

Tini shot forward, his wings a blur of movement. The heat pressed against him like a giant's breath, thick and suffocating. Sparks swirled in the air, and smoke choked the sky, turning daylight into an eerie, flickering twilight. He reached the edge of a burning tree, where flames licked the bark like hungry tongues. Without hesitation, he dove toward the stream, scooped up a tiny droplet of water in his beak, and zipped back to the fire.

With a fierce determination, he let the drop fall onto the flames. The fire hissed, barely noticing the tiny offering. Tini did it again. And again. And again. His body screamed for rest, but he would not stop. He zipped back and forth, faster than he ever had before, carrying drop after drop, even as the fire continued its relentless march.

From the trees above, the animals watched in stunned silence. The jaguar, mighty and fierce, stood frozen. The capybara, wise and calm, trembled. Even the great condors, who ruled the sky, did not know what to do. But Tini, the smallest of them all, was fighting alone.

The fire raged on. The jungle, once alive with song, was now filled with cries of terror and the endless roar of destruction. Tini's wings ached. His breath came in short, ragged bursts. His feathers were singed, and his vision swam from the rising heat. But still, he kept going.

And then something changed. A single monkey, swinging low from the trees, saw the hummingbird's struggle. He scooped up a large leaf, dripping with water, and swung over the flames, shaking the droplets loose.

A jaguar, watching from the shadows, took a deep breath and used his mighty tail to slap dirt onto the flames.

A tapir, huge and strong, charged into the shallows of the river, soaking its thick skin before rolling onto the burning undergrowth.

The ants, small but mighty, carried dew in their tiny jaws. The parrots, squawking war cries, beat their wings against the smoke to clear a path.

Even the great anaconda, slow and silent, slithered through the wreckage, smothering flames beneath its massive coils.

The animals of the jungle, once frozen by fear, now fought together. And little by little, the fire began to lose its grip.

It took all night, but by dawn, the fire was dying. The once-raging inferno had been tamed. Smoke still curled into the sky, and the jungle lay in blackened ruin, but it was not gone. Green still peeked through the ashes. The trees, wounded but standing, whispered of rebirth. The animals, weary and covered in soot, gathered in the clearing. They looked at Tini, who sat perched on a charred branch, his feathers dulled but his spirit unbroken.

Then, the great jaguar stepped forward. "You, little one, are the bravest of us all."

A deep murmur of agreement rippled through the crowd. The parrots chirped their praise. The monkeys whooped and cheered. Even the silent owls, who rarely spoke, nodded solemnly.

Tini, exhausted, simply smiled. "I am only small," he said softly. "But the jungle is our home. And we all must fight for what we love."

The jungle remembered. Tini's name was whispered in the rustling of the leaves, sung by the birds at dawn, and carried on the winds that swept through the mountains. And when, years later, another fire threatened the forest, the animals did not hesitate. They remembered the little hummingbird, and they fought. For courage, after all, is not measured in size. It is measured in heart.

Legend Of The Callejón Del Armado

This story has been adapted from a tale originally told by Thomas A. Janvier in Legends Of The City Of Mexico, published in 1910 by Harper & Brothers Publishers, New York. Legends of the City of Mexico delves into the rich cultural heritage of Mexico, exploring the myths and legends that have been passed down through generations. The book included a diverse range of stories, drawing from Aztec, Spanish, and indigenous Mexican traditions.

The Alleyway of the Armed One earned its name long ago, before it had any name at all, when an old man lived there, always dressed in armour and carrying both a sword and a dagger at his side. All that was known about him was that his name was Don Lope de Armijo y Lara. Despite living in a poor, run-down street in one of the city's roughest quarters, he was a wealthy merchant from Spain.

No one had ever set foot inside his humble house. He lived entirely alone, surrounded by an air of secrecy. Despite his great wealth, he had no servants, buying his own food and cooking with his own hands.

Whenever he ventured outside, he was always armed to the teeth (armado hasta los dientes). Beneath his plain, tattered robe, he wore a full suit of armour. His belt carried a long dagger and a broad sword, and when he left the house at night, he would take a great pike with him.

Soon, people stopped calling him Don Lope and instead referred to him simply as "El Armado", The Armed One.

It was widely believed that El Armado was a wicked man, yet he was strangely devoted to charity. Each morning, he would pray for hours at the church of San Francisco, kneeling humbly as if seeking forgiveness. He was known to receive the Sacrament at the proper times, and some claimed that, at night, through the shuttered windows of his house, they could hear the sound of him scourging himself in penance.

Whenever the darkest, stormiest nights descended, especially those with a cold, relentless drizzle, he would be seen leaving his house, fully armed, making his way towards the Plazuela de Mixcalco. He would disappear into the shadows and not return until after midnight.

Once back in his house, the sounds of coins clinking would echo through the walls, counting, counting, always counting, as though his wealth had no end. Then, as the coin-counting stopped, the sound of a whip would follow, accompanied by groans of agony. Finally, a heavy clanking would be heard, the unmistakable crash of a great iron lid slamming shut upon an iron chest.

After that, silence. Not a sign of life until morning, when the Armed One would emerge once again and return to San Francisco to pray.

People whispered about his secret life, some wishing to expose his crimes by reporting him to the authorities. Yet, in the end, his fate revealed itself without anyone's intervention, and in the strangest way imaginable. One morning, the neighbours awoke to a terrifying sight. The Armed One was hanging dead from his own balcony, a rope around his neck!

No one could understand what had happened. Had he taken his own life in fear of being exposed? Had he been haunted by guilt? Had justice finally caught up with him in some unknowable way?

When the Alcalde arrived to investigate, they searched his house and discovered a vast fortune hidden within its walls. But far more chillingly, they also found numerous human skulls, gruesome evidence that many had met their end at his hands.

El Chupacabra

This story is my own adaptation of a traditional regional tale. This version is based on sources from Puerto Rico and Mexico.

The jungle of Tierra Verde was ancient, its roots entangled with stories as old as time itself. Its trees stood taller than kings, their gnarled branches woven into an emerald canopy that filtered the golden sunlight into fragments of green and gold.

But in the undergrowth, where shadows slithered between the ferns and the vines whispered secrets to one another, there lurked something far older than the trees. A creature of night and legend.

The elders called it El Chupacabra, the Blood Drinker. Its name carried a terror that made even the bravest hunters hesitate.

"Do not stray beyond the river at night," the villagers would warn. Do not wander too far into the heart of the jungle, for that is where El Chupacabra watches. And should you cross its path, you will never return."

Some claimed that the creature was a demon, a beast of fangs and claws, prowling the jungle in search of blood. Others swore that it was a guardian, a guard sent by the old spirits to defend the wild against those who would desecrate its sacred ground. None truly knew.

Then, one fateful night, a man named Carlos ventured into the jungle alone, seeking fortune, glory, and a truth far greater than he could have imagined.

Carlos was no fool. He had heard the stories since he was a child, whispered over campfires and carried on the breath of the wind. But he was not one to be ruled by fear. He was an adventurer, a seeker of wonders. For years, he had explored the lost corners of the world, uncovering ruins swallowed by the jungle, forgotten maps, and artifacts older than memory. Yet no treasure had ever quenched his hunger. He still sought something greater than gold, for he scoured the corners of the earth for legend.

And so, when Carlos heard of El Chupacabra, he could not resist the lure of the unknown. "Find the beast," he had told himself. "Face it. Learn its secret. Become legend yourself."

With nothing but his machete, a lantern, and the fire of curiosity burning in his chest, he ventured into the depths of Tierra Verde, following the whispers of the jungle.

The jungle at night was a world of its own. It was alive, breathing, watching. The leaves trembled with unseen movement, and the air hummed with an eerie melody, the chitter of insects, the distant hoot of an owl, the slow, deliberate rustle of something large moving just beyond sight.

Carlos felt a thousand unseen eyes upon his every movement. Then, as if summoned by the will of the earth, he stepped into a clearing bathed in moonlight. And there it was. El Chupacabra.

The creature was a shadow darker than the night itself. Its eyes smouldered red, reflecting the glow of the moon. Its form was twisted, and unnatural, a creature of grace and menace. Muscles coiled beneath its obsidian skin, and when it moved, it was silent as the wind, yet each step rippled through the air like a storm about to break.

Carlos should have run, but instead, he stood frozen, caught between terror and wonder.

The creature studied him, head tilting ever so slightly.

Carlos, summoning every ounce of courage, spoke in a voice barely above a whisper. "Why do you haunt these jungles, El Chupacabra?"

The air grew thicker, charged with something ancient and powerful.

Then, to his utter astonishment, the beast answered. "I do not haunt," the voice rumbled. It was deep, like the distant roll of thunder, ancient as the stones buried beneath the roots of the jungle. "I guard."

Carlos's breath caught in his throat. "Guard what?" he asked.

El Chupacabra's gaze did not waver. The shadows around them deepened, and Carlos felt as though the jungle itself was listening.

"The old ones," the creature said. "The spirits that sleep beneath the roots. The blood of the jungle, the breath of the world. I was made to keep the balance, to stop those who seek to take what is not theirs."

Carlos felt his heart pound. He had come seeking a beast, but he had found a guardian of something far greater than mere legend.

"And what do you see me as?" Carlos asked, voice shaking.

The creature watched him for a long moment. Then, with slow, deliberate steps, El Chupacabra circled him, its presence as vast as the sky. "I see a man standing at a crossroad," it murmured. "One path leads forward. The other leads back. And your choice will shape more than just yourself."

Carlos felt a shiver crawl down his spine. "What must I do?" he whispered.

El Chupacabra lowered its head, bringing its glowing eyes level with Carlos's own. "You are no enemy of the jungle," it said. "Not yet. But the world of men is filled with hunger. It takes. It scars. It burns. I have seen it before, and I will see it again."

The wind howled through the trees, as if lamenting the truth of its words.

"If you wish to walk forward," the guardian said, "then swear it here. Swear to protect this land. Swear to listen to its whispers, to shield its secrets from those who would exploit them. Swear it, and you shall not walk alone."

Carlos took a deep breath. He had sought treasure, but he had found purpose. He had hunted legend, but he had found something greater than mere game. Dropping to one knee, he pressed his hand to the earth, feeling the heartbeat of the jungle beneath his palm.

"I swear it."

A ripple passed through the trees, as if the forest had accepted his oath.

El Chupacabra nodded once. "Then you are bound to the jungle, as it is bound to you."

From that night on, Carlos's name was spoken with growing reverence. He became a protector, a guide, a voice for the spirits of Tierra Verde. And when the fires came, when men with axes and machines sought to claim the land for their own, they found their paths blocked. Their tools broken. Their footprints erased. For the jungle had more guardians now.

And somewhere, beneath the ancient canopy, a pair of red eyes still watch, ever vigilant. El Chupacabra, once feared, now stands as the eternal sentinel of the wild. The legend lives on.

Legend Of The Aduana De Santo Domingo

This story has been adapted from a tale originally told by Thomas A. Janvier in Legends Of The City Of Mexico, published in 1910 by Harper & Brothers Publishers, New York. Legends of the City of Mexico delves into the rich cultural heritage of Mexico, exploring the myths and legends that have been passed down through generations. The book included a diverse range of stories, drawing from Aztec, Spanish, and indigenous Mexican traditions.

The gentleman who, for the sake of love, overcame his cold and lethargic nature to become a man of fire and energy was Don Juan Gutiérrez Rubín de Celis. He was a knight of the Order of Santiago, though some claimed he also wore the habit of Calatrava, and served as colonel of the Tres Villas regiment.

By nature, he was charming, ostentatious, and arrogant, but also infamously slow and indifferent in all matters. His wealth was so immense that even he did not know the full extent of it. To illustrate his extravagance, on one particular state occasion in 1716, when the new Viceroy, the Marqués de Valero, made his grand entrance into the city, Don Juan adorned his coat with pearls worth thirty thousand pesos, purely as decoration.

By that time, Don Juan must have been in his forties, still in his prime, when the event that changed everything occurred. He fell madly in love. This sudden and overwhelming passion was the first true sign of energy he had ever displayed in his life.

The object of his intense affection was the young and beautiful Doña Sara de García Somera y Acuña. She was less than half his age, yet possessed a sharp mind and a thoughtful nature that set her apart from most young women. She came from a noble family and was a blood relative of the Viceroy, who by that time was Don Juan de Acuña, Marqués de Casafuerte. Given his close ties to both parties, the Viceroy took great interest in this unfolding romance.

Don Juan's courtship of Doña Sara did not proceed smoothly, as she was not one to act impulsively. She considered the situation carefully and rationally, weighing the advantages and disadvantages of marrying him. On one hand, she found him dull and apathetic, and he was old enough to be her father, hardly an ideal match for a passionate young woman. On the other hand, his title and immense wealth made him one of the most influential figures in the Vice-Kingdom. Furthermore, despite his age, he was still an attractive and distinguished man.

Her conflicted feelings left her unable to decide.

While Don Juan was desperately in love, and Doña Sara was weighing her options, an event occurred that shifted the course of their relationship. The Viceroy, who was both a friend to Don Juan and a relative of Doña Sara, appointed Don Juan as the Prior of the Consulado, the President of the Tribunal of Commerce. This was a prestigious role, perfectly suited to his rank and fortune. Even better, it was a position that required almost no effort, since all duties could be delegated to deputies or even left undone entirely, making it an ideal match for Don Juan's natural laziness.

At the time, the Aduana de Santo Domingo (the Santo Domingo Customs House) was under construction, a project that had been moving at a painfully slow pace for years. The Consulado was responsible for overseeing its completion, but successive Priors had done little to speed things along. Don Juan, the new Prior, was more than content to continue this tradition of inaction.

It was at this moment that Doña Sara conceived a brilliant plan, one that would determine whether Don Juan's lazy apathy was truly ingrained or if, beneath his passion for her, there was a hidden well of energy she could awaken and channel into productive work. Her reasoning was simple. If she could inspire him to undertake real, vigorous work, then it was likely she could also drive him out of his idleness entirely, transforming him into the kind of husband she desired.

And so, Doña Sara set Don Juan a single condition for their marriage. He must complete the long-delayed construction of the Aduana within six months.

Blinded by his overwhelming love for Doña Sara, Don Juan accepted her challenge without hesitation. This man, who had never lifted a finger in his entire life, promised her that he would achieve what seemed impossible, that he would complete the Aduana within six months!

The entire city was astonished, and, truth be told, so was Don Juan himself, at the fierce determination with which he set about his task. In an instant, he summoned every architect in the city, pleading with them to oversee the construction. But they all told him the same thing. "Not even a miracle could complete such a task in six months!"

With no one willing to take on the challenge, Don Juan did something even more extraordinary, he took charge of the entire project himself. And the raging passion that had fuelled his love for Doña Sara now ignited his ambition.

From that moment on, it was as though tempests and volcanoes raged within Don Juan. He summoned thousands of labourers from the Tierra Caliente, magically mobilising an army of workers to dig and carry heavy loads. He filled every quarry around the city with stone-cutters, ensuring that construction materials were never in short supply. Then he put every mason to work laying the walls, every carpenter to crafting doors and windows, every brickmaker to producing tiles for the roof and floors, and every blacksmith to forging locks, hinges, window grilles, and balcony railings.

And Don Juan himself worked harder than all of them put together. He was everywhere at once, driving them on, demanding speed and efficiency. Any worker who even hesitated for a moment faced a storm of curses from Don Juan's lips, his words sharp as scorpions, vipers, and toads!

Yet, despite his frenzied pace, there was no madness in his methods. Every moment was optimised, every task meticulously planned. Not a second was wasted, and before the city's very eyes, the Aduana began to rise. Don Juan had made up his whole soul to succeed, and succeed he did.

Three full days before the deadline, the Aduana stood complete, finished down to the last detail. Triumphant, Don Juan carried the key to the magnificent building to the Palace and personally placed it in the hands of the Viceroy. But his greatest achievement was yet to be revealed.

To ensure the entire world knew why and for whom he had completed this seemingly impossible feat, Don Juan had an inscription carved into one of the Aduana's walls. At first glance, it seemed like a simple dedication, just his name, the names of the consuls, and the date of completion. But in truth, the first letters of each of the five lines spelt out Doña Sara's initials, a hidden tribute to the woman who had inspired him to greatness.

With his task completed, Don Juan had proven beyond doubt that, beneath his former apathy, lay an unstoppable force of energy, enough to outmatch fifty ordinary men.

And so, Doña Sara was well satisfied. If her influence had driven him to such astonishing achievements, then surely it would continue to shape him into the perfect husband. Without hesitation, she married Don Juan.

And today the Aduana still stands, precisely where Don Juan built it in record time. If you doubt the truth of this tale, you need only look at the building, and read the hidden inscription with Doña Sara's initials, proof that her choice of husband was, indeed, well made.

La Tulivieja

This story is my own adaptation of a traditional regional tale. This version is based on Colombian and Panamanian sources.

The villagers never spoke her name above a whisper…

In the heart of Colombia, where the mountains clawed at the sky and the valleys lay drenched in an eternal sea of mist, there was a tale older than memory, a tale of sorrow and ruin, of vanity turned to horror. It was the legend of La Tulivieja.

In the daylight, the villagers kept busy, tending to their crops, guiding their herds through the rolling hills, weaving stories into tapestries of the mundane. But when night fell, when the lanterns flickered and the wind whispered through the hollow spaces between trees, the world changed. For in the shadows of the ancient forests, something watched and waited.

And those foolish enough to wander alone after sundown would hear it first, a wretched, weeping cry, tangled in the howling wind. "Where is my beauty?"

The question was always the same. A voice thick with grief, with rage, with an unholy hunger. The elders warned: Do not answer. Do not follow, for La Tulivieja does not forgive.

Before she became a terror of the night, before she was a creature of ruin, she was a woman so beautiful that the air trembled around her. Her name had been lost to time, buried beneath the savagery of her legend, but she had once been a lady of splendour, her raven-black hair cascading down her back, her eyes like stolen stars, and her smile a weapon as sharp as any dagger.

Men adored her. Men worshipped her. She took their love with a smirk, casting them aside like petals plucked from a dying flower. The young men of the village fought for her favour, while their mothers cursed her name beneath their breath, calling her vain, shallow, wicked. She did not care. The world was hers to play with. Until one fateful night, when she laid her eyes upon the landowner, Don Sebastián Monteverde.

Don Sebastián Monteverde was a man of wealth, power, and sin. He was a man with a wife who loved him, and a child who bore his name, but none of that mattered to her. She wanted him. And what La Tulivieja wanted, she took.

Their affair was passionate, reckless, and damned from the start. For months, they met in secret, behind the churchyard at midnight, in the abandoned mill by the river, in the shadowed corridors of his grand estate when his wife was away.

The village whispered.

His wife wept.

And when the truth could no longer be hidden, the heavens themselves raged.

On a night when the moon bled red, when the sky churned with storm clouds and thunder cracked like a god's fury, Doña Isabela Monteverde cursed the woman who had stolen her husband. Her voice rose with the storm, her sobs shaking the earth, as she called upon the spirits of the land, the restless dead, the ancient forces that slumbered beneath the soil. "Take her beauty, take her soul…let her suffer as I have suffered. Let her be forsaken by love, by life, by death itself."

In that moment the ground split open beneath La Tulivieja's feet, and the night swallowed her whole.

She awoke in darkness. Something was wrong. Her skin crawled, stretched too tight over bones that no longer felt human. Her fingers were elongated and twisted into talons, each nail blackened like the charred remains of a cold funeral pyre. Her lips were cracked, her mouth dry with thirst. Her face…oh, her face.

She dragged herself toward the river, her body moving awkwardly, wrongly, her steps a shambling nightmare. When she looked into the water, she screamed. The reflection that stared back was monstrous, a face distorted by agony, her once radiant eyes now sunken and hollow, her beauty stolen, replaced by something grotesque, something inhuman. She tore at her hair, at her skin, but the curse had bound itself to her bones.

And then, from the depths of her despair, came the hunger, a hunger that gnawed at her insides, a hunger that no food, no water, no light could satisfy. It was a hunger for something else entirely. Blood and life.

And so, La Tulivieja rose from the river, her body a shadow against the moonlit fog, and she began to hunt.

Her curse bound her to eternal sorrow. She could not find peace, nor could she ever rest. And so, she wandered, through forests and valleys, across rivers and mountains, her wretched wail echoing through the night.

"Where is my beauty?"

The villagers locked their doors. Children hid beneath their blankets. And those foolish enough to answer her cry, to step into the night and offer their voice to the darkness never returned. For La Tulivieja did not kill quickly.

She would lure them in, her voice soft and desperate, her silhouette a pitiful figure in the mist. But once they drew close enough to see her face, once they saw the rotting horror that she had become, it was too late. Her talons would pierce their skin. Her breath, as cold as the grave, would steal the warmth from their veins. She would drink their life away, drop by drop, until all that remained was a hollow husk, that would drift away on a whisper of wind among the trees.

La Tulivieja will never be free. Her torment is endless. She will wander until the stars themselves burn to cinders, seeking beauty and love that can never be hers, hungering for what she can never have again.

Villagers will continue to fear the night, and to whisper her name in hushed, trembling voices. They will warn their children:

"Stay on the path."

"Never answer the weeping woman."

"Do not look for La Tulivieja, for she is already looking for you."

Somewhere, in the mist-covered valleys of Colombia, where the wind carries the echoes of long-forgotten sins, a voice will rise, a voice that is neither alive nor dead, a voice that will never stop crying.

"Where …?"

Legend Of The Calle De La Quemada

This story has been adapted from a tale originally told by Thomas A. Janvier in Legends Of The City Of Mexico, published in 1910 by Harper & Brothers Publishers, New York. Legends of the City of Mexico delves into the rich cultural heritage of Mexico, exploring the myths and legends that have been passed down through generations. The book included a diverse range of stories, drawing from Aztec, Spanish, and indigenous Mexican traditions.

Many people, without knowing the truth, will tell you that the Street of the Burned Woman got its name because, during the time when the Holy Office of the Inquisition was at its height, purging the wicked to aid the righteous, a heretical woman was burned there.

This, however, is completely false. The Quemadero of the Inquisition, where such executions took place, was located at the western end of what is now the Alameda, far from Calle de la Quemada. The real story behind the name is far more tragic, for it was a beautiful young woman who set fire to her own face, deliberately destroying her beauty to resolve the doubts in her heart.

This event took place during the reign of the noble Viceroy Don Luis de Velasco, meaning this tale is now over three hundred years old.

The young woman in question was Doña Beatrice de Espinosa, daughter of Don Gonzalo de Espinosa y Guevara, a wealthy Spanish merchant who had travelled to New Spain to expand his fortune. Upon settling, he took up residence in San Pablo, on what would later become the Street of the Burned Woman.

Doña Beatrice was said to be as beautiful as the moon and stars combined, yet she was also even more virtuous than she was beautiful. At twenty years old, she was the envy of every noble family in the city. All the young men fell in love with her, and many wealthy and aristocratic suitors, through their families, sought her father's permission to marry her.

However, Doña Beatrice was highly selective, and not a single one of these suitors pleased her. Respecting her wishes, her father turned them all away. That was, until one fateful night.

At a grand ball held at the Viceroy's palace, Doña Beatrice finally found what her heart had been waiting for, a noble Italian gentleman named Don Martín Scipoli, the Marquess of Pinamonte y Frantescello.

Like all the others before him, Don Martín fell instantly in love with Doña Beatrice. But unlike any other man before him, she fell in love with him too.

Don Martín was handsome, passionate, and utterly devoted, but also extremely jealous and dangerously quarrelsome. Soon, his love for Beatrice ignited violent conflicts across the city. Overcome with jealousy at the mere thought of her past admirers, he provoked duels with them at every opportunity, seeking satisfaction at the point of his sword.

Doña Beatrice, however, was deeply troubled. To her, love was pure and spiritual, much like that of angels. She feared that Don Martín's love was not for her soul, but only for her beauty. She also agonised over the suffering he caused, wounding and even killing young men out of jealousy for a love she had already given him freely.

After much prayer and reflection, she resolved to destroy her own beauty, so that Don Martín could no longer be blinded by her appearance, and she could know, once and for all, whether his love was truly soul for soul.

One evening, while her father was away from home, she sent all the servants out on various errands. Left alone, she lit a brazier of burning coals in her chamber and placed it beneath an image of Saint Lucia, the patron saint of sight and divine clarity. Saint Lucia had, after all, famously plucked out her own beautiful eyes and sent them to a suitor who had distracted her from her devotion, saying that since he claimed he could not live without them, he may as well have them.

Beatrice did not intend to follow Saint Lucia's example completely, however. Unlike the saint, she needed to keep her eyes so that she could witness Don Martín's reaction. So, she covered them with a damp handkerchief, ensuring she would be able to see the truth, and then fanned the flames until the brazier glowed fiercely. Then, without hesitation, she thrust her face into the fire.

It was at that very moment, though she could not have known, that the street outside was given its infamous name.

Once the agony of the burns had subsided, Doña Beatrice summoned Don Martín. She met him dressed in pure white, a veil covering her ruined face. She said nothing as she slowly lifted the veil, revealing what remained of her once extraordinary beauty. What Don Martín saw was worse than anything he had ever imagined.

Her two brilliant eyes remained untouched, but the rest of her face was a twisted, scarred ruin. The contrast between the living, shining eyes and the burned, lifeless skin was so ghastly that he shuddered in horror. But instead of rejecting her, he was overcome with love and gratitude.

At once, he married her, embracing her not for her outer beauty, but for the soul he had always loved. From that day forward, his love was no longer for her face, but for her very essence.

Her sacrifice became legend, and her street, the Street of the Burned Woman, will forever remind us that true love should be for the soul, not for the face.

Hen And Coyote

This story is my own adaptation of a traditional regional tale. This tale is based on Honduran sources.

Once upon a time, in the ancient land of the Maya, there lived a mischievous hen and a cunning coyote. They were known throughout the land for their cleverness and their ability to outwit even the most formidable opponents.

The hen and the coyote were constant companions, always getting into mischief together. They roamed the forests and fields, seeking adventure and excitement wherever they went. Despite their differences in size and appearance, they were the best of friends, relying on each other for companionship and support.

One day, as they were wandering through the forest in search of food, they stumbled upon a lush mango tree heavy with ripe fruit. The hen, with her keen eyesight, spotted the mangoes first and eagerly plucked one from the tree, her beak watering at the thought of the sweet flesh inside.

But before she could take a single bite, the coyote intervened, his eyes gleaming with greed. "Wait, my friend," he said slyly. "Let us first see if these mangoes are ripe enough to eat."

With that, the coyote picked up a fallen mango from the ground and tossed it high into the air. The mango landed with a soft thud, its skin splitting open to reveal the golden flesh inside. "Ah, it seems ripe enough," declared the coyote with a grin. "Now we can enjoy our feast."

But as the hen reached out to take another mango from the tree, disaster struck. The branch she was perched on snapped beneath her weight, sending her tumbling to the ground below. The coyote watched in horror as his friend crashed to the forest floor, her wings flapping frantically as she struggled to right herself.

Without hesitation, the coyote sprang into action, darting forward to rescue the hen from danger. With his sharp teeth and nimble paws, he quickly scooped her up and carried her to safety, his heart pounding with fear for his beloved friend.

From that day forward, the hen and the coyote were inseparable, their bond stronger than ever. They continued to roam the forests and fields together, facing whatever challenges came their way with courage and determination.

And though they may have been an unlikely pair, the hen and the coyote proved that true friendship knows no bounds, transcending differences in size, shape, and species. Together, they were unstoppable, their adventures the stuff of legend in the ancient land of the Maya.

Legend Of The Calle De La Cruz Verde

This story has been adapted from a tale originally told by Thomas A. Janvier in Legends Of The City Of Mexico, published in 1910 by Harper & Brothers Publishers, New York. Legends of the City of Mexico delves into the rich cultural heritage of Mexico, exploring the myths and legends that have been passed down through generations. The book included a diverse range of stories, drawing from Aztec, Spanish, and indigenous Mexican traditions.

This is a joyful story of a gentleman and a lady who fell in love, married, and lived happily together until the end of their days. And it was in gratitude for his happiness that the gentleman had a great green stone cross carved onto the corner of his house, just below the balcony where he first saw the sign that gave him hope. That cross still stands today.

The house with the green cross is located at the corner of Calle de la Cruz Verde, named after it, and Calle de Migueles. When Doña María's father built it, it was a grand residence, though it has since grown old and worn. The saint that once stood in the niche above the cross is long gone, but in its place, there is now a fine pulquería, La Heroína, where one can find the freshest pulque every morning, all year round.

Don Álvaro de Villadiego y Manrique, the gentleman in question, arrived in Mexico in the service of Viceroy Don Gastón de Peralta. If that is true, then it must have happened a very long time ago. Don Álvaro was a striking figure, tall, slender, and fair, with golden-brown hair and a neatly pointed beard. He wore white velvet robes embroidered with gold, a blue cap with a white feather, and always rode a magnificent Arabian horse.

One day, while riding through Calle de Migueles, he was dressed in his finest attire, for there was a festival in the city. As he pranced down the street on his noble steed, his eyes fell upon a beautiful young lady standing on the balcony of a grand house, the same house where the green cross now stands.

She was elegant and graceful, her skin as fair as snow, and in that instant, Don Álvaro fell hopelessly in love with her. Though she was too well-mannered to show it, Doña María de Aldarafuente y Segura felt the same way.

Determined to win her hand, Don Álvaro rode past her balcony every day, gazing up at her with eyes full of love. However, Doña María had been raised with great discipline, and her parents watched her closely, so for a long time, she gave no sign that she had noticed him at all. But the longer she was forced to remain silent, the deeper her love for him grew.

Eventually, Doña María's mother fell ill, and with the household in distress, her family's watch over her became less strict. It was then that Don Álvaro saw his chance. He sent her a letter, begging her to declare her love for him. In the letter, he gave her two choices: If she did not love him, she should hang a cross made of dry palm leaves from her balcony. Upon seeing this, he swore that he would die that very day. If she did love him, she should hang a cross made of fresh green palm leaves, a sign that she had given him her promise of eternal happiness.

Being a lady of dignity, Doña María waited several days before responding. Each passing moment drove Don Álvaro to the brink of madness. The uncertainty consumed him, and his mind was so close to breaking that one more day of silence would have driven him insane.

Then, on a beautiful spring morning, as the sun shone brightly and birds filled the air with song, Don Álvaro looked up to the balcony, and there, hanging from the railing, was a radiant green cross.

From that moment, everything fell into place. A respected cleric, who was a friend of both Don Álvaro and Doña María's family, acted as their intermediary. He arranged the match with such diplomacy and skill that within two weeks, though to Don Álvaro, the wait felt endless, the couple stood together before the altar, vowing eternal love to one another. And, best of all, they remained true to their vow.

To commemorate their happiness, Don Álvaro commissioned a large green stone cross to be carved into the corner of their home, the same house they shared for the rest of their lives. The cross was placed beneath the balcony where Doña María had once hung the green palm cross, the symbol of her promise of eternal love.

To this day, the green cross still stands, and the street was named Calle de la Cruz Verde in its honour, which, as I'm sure you will agree, proves that this story is absolutely true.

The Exquisite Quetzal

This story is my own adaptation of a traditional regional tale. This tale is based on Guatemalan sources.

Once upon a time, in the verdant forests of Guatemala, there lived a magnificent bird known as the Quetzal. Its feathers shimmered with iridescent greens, blues, and reds, like precious jewels gleaming in the sunlight. The Quetzal was revered by the ancient Maya people, who considered it a symbol of divinity and freedom.

Legend had it that the Quetzal possessed magical powers, and whoever caught sight of its elusive beauty was said to be blessed with good fortune. But despite its mystical allure, the Quetzal was a solitary creature, preferring the solitude of the forest to the company of others.

One day, a humble woodcutter named Juan ventured deep into the heart of the forest in search of firewood. As he wandered among the towering trees, he heard a melodious song echoing through the branches, a song so sweet and enchanting that it seemed to beckon him closer.

Curious, Juan followed the sound until he came upon a clearing bathed in golden sunlight. There, perched upon a moss-covered branch, was the most exquisite bird he had ever seen, It was the Quetzal. Its feathers shimmered in the dappled light, casting a rainbow of colours across the forest floor.

Mesmerized by the bird's beauty, Juan approached slowly, his heart pounding with wonder and awe. But as he drew near, the Quetzal took flight, its wings beating gracefully as it soared into the sky.

Determined to capture the bird's beauty forever, Juan set out to find the perfect gift to offer the Quetzal in exchange for its feathers. He searched high and low, gathering rare flowers, precious gems, and shimmering jewels from the forest floor.

At last, Juan returned to the clearing, his arms laden with treasures beyond compare. With trembling hands, he offered his gifts to the Quetzal, hoping to win its favour and earn a single feather as a token of its grace. To his surprise, the Quetzal accepted Juan's offerings, its eyes sparkling with curiosity and amusement. With a graceful flick of its tail, the bird plucked a single feather from its wing and placed it in Juan's outstretched hand.

Overwhelmed with gratitude, Juan thanked the Quetzal and vowed to cherish the feather for all eternity. As he journeyed home, the forest seemed to come alive with the colours of the Quetzal's plumage, filling his heart with joy and wonder.

From that day forward, Juan treasured the Quetzal's feather as a reminder of the beauty and magic that dwelled within the heart of the forest. And though he never saw the bird again, its song echoed in his memories, a testament to the timeless allure of the Exquisite Quetzal.

Legend Of La Mujer Herrada

This story has been adapted from a tale originally told by Thomas A. Janvier in Legends Of The City Of Mexico, published in 1910 by Harper & Brothers Publishers, New York. Legends of the City of Mexico delves into the rich cultural heritage of Mexico, exploring the myths and legends that have been passed down through generations. The book included a diverse range of stories, drawing from Aztec, Spanish, and indigenous Mexican traditions.

A priest and his housekeeper lived in a house on Puerta Falsa de Santo Domingo, though that house no longer stands. A blacksmith, lived in a house on Calle de las Rejas de la Balvanera, and above its doorway, there was a farrier's knife and a pair of pincers carved into the stone arch.

The priest was a secular clergyman, not belonging to any religious order, and he and the blacksmith were compadres, that is, close friends. The blacksmith, having a great respect and affection for his friend, often advised him to send his housekeeper away. But the priest always found an excuse to keep her, and so the matter was put off for years.

One night, the blacksmith was abruptly woken from his sleep by loud banging at his door. When he got up to see who it was, he found two men standing outside, strangers he had never seen before, and with them was a she-mule they had brought to be shod.

The men apologised for disturbing him at such an unholy hour and explained that the mule belonged to his compadre, the priest. They said the priest was leaving on an urgent journey the following morning and needed the mule shod immediately.

The blacksmith examined the animal closely and saw that, indeed, it belonged to his friend. So, as a favour, he fitted the mule with new iron shoes.

When the job was done, the two men led the mule away. But as they disappeared into the dark streets, they began beating the poor creature mercilessly with heavy sticks. The blacksmith, shocked by their brutality, shouted at them to stop, but they ignored him. Even after they vanished into the darkness, he could still hear the awful sound of their blows.

Something about the whole incident troubled the blacksmith deeply. So, at the first light of morning, he went straight to his compadre's house, intending to ask him why he had sent those men and what journey required such urgency. However, when he arrived, he was kept waiting for some time before the priest finally opened the door, looking half-asleep. When asked about his unexpected trip, the priest laughed in confusion, for he had no plans to go anywhere and had certainly not sent his mule to be shod.

As he woke up properly, he found the whole thing hilarious, teasing the blacksmith for falling for such a trick. Wanting to share the joke, he called out to his housekeeper, knocking on her door. But she did not respond. He knocked again, louder this time, but there was still, no reply. Suddenly, the two men grew anxious. Together, they forced open the door and stepped inside.

What they found froze them in horror, for it was the most terrible sight that either of them had ever seen. Lying on the bed, twisted in agony, was the lifeless body of the housekeeper. Her hands and feet had been nailed into iron horseshoes, the very same ones the blacksmith had fitted onto the mule's hooves the night before. Worse still, her body was covered in bruises and welts, marks left by the savage beatings inflicted by the two strangers. And the woman was dead beyond doubt.

At once, the two men understood the dreadful truth. This was no ordinary event. The two men had not been men at all but demons in disguise. They had transformed the housekeeper into a mule and taken her to be shod as punishment for her sins.

Realising his grave mistake, the priest fled his house, vanishing without a trace, never to be seen or heard from again. As for the blacksmith, the guilt weighed on him for the rest of his life. Though he had been unknowingly deceived, he could never shake the memory of what he had done. Until the day he died, he lived in sorrow, haunted by the terrifying fate of the Iron-Shod Woman.

The Legend of Turrialba

This story is my own adaptation of a traditional regional tale. This tale is based on Costa Rican sources.

The valley of Turrialba was a land of eternal mist, where the earth exhaled whispers of primordial power, and the towering volcano loomed like a sleeping giant, its breath curling in tendrils of smoke from its gaping mouth.

At the heart of this land, among lush forests and fertile fields, stood a great stone fortress, the domain of Chief Curubandá, ruler of the indigenous tribe that had called these lands home for generations. And in this fortress lived his daughter, the radiant Princess Turrialba.

She was a creature of light, yet she belonged to the darkness of the mountain's looming shadow. Her beauty was spoken of in hushed, reverent voices, as if she were not of mortal flesh, but a spirit woven from moonlight and mist. Her hair, dark as obsidian, cascaded down her back in waves, and her eyes gleamed like the reflection of fire upon water.

But it was not only her beauty that set her apart, but it was also her kindness, her wisdom, her voice like the first rains of the season. She moved among her people with grace, yet something always lingered behind her gaze, as though she heard things that others could not, or saw the shadows moving in the smoke rising from the mountain's peak.

She was loved, but she was also feared, for the volcano had always been a god unto itself, and some whispered that it had chosen her.

Though many sought Turrialba's hand, she remained untouched by their affections. She did not desire gold or warriors, nor the promises of power. Her heart belonged to Izel, a humble farmer whose hands knew only the rich, dark soil of the valley. He was not a man of great wealth or legend, but his spirit was gentle, steadfast, and when Turrialba was with him, the mountain was silent, as though, for a time, it did not dare to breathe. But peace is a thing never left untouched for long.

One fateful evening, under the light of a dying sun, a shadow entered the valley. His name was Xelhua, a warrior of a distant tribe, a man as relentless as the rising tide, his armour blackened with the blood of those who had stood against him. He came with lavish gifts, with promises of power, with a hunger in his eyes that made even the trees blush.

"Take me as your husband," he said, his voice a blade wrapped in silk.

But Turrialba did not waver. "My heart is not mine to give," she said, and turned away.

Xelhua's eyes darkened. His pride, his unstoppable force, had never before met an immovable object. And so, in his rage, he sought to break what he could not claim.

The challenge was set. A duel between Xelhua and Izel, between a warrior born of war and a man who knew only the earth. No one believed it would be a contest of equals. And indeed, it was not.

Under the blood-red sky, the battle began. Izel fought bravely, but bravery is not steel. Xelhua struck him down, the cruel edge of his obsidian blade slicing through muscle and bone, leaving Izel broken upon the ground, gasping like an animal caught in the jaws of a wolf.

Turrialba cried out, her voice tearing through the air like a lament carried on the wind. She rushed to his side, pressing her trembling hands to his wound, but it was too deep. The earth trembled beneath them. And then, Turrialba did something that would change the course of the valley's fate forever.

She lifted her tear-streaked face to the heavens, her eyes burning with a fire that rivalled the sun itself, and she called to the gods of the volcano. "Take me instead!" she cried. "Spare him, and I will give myself to you!"

Her voice was a song of sacrifice, carried into the heart of the mountain. And the gods listened.

The moment the words left her lips, the sky cracked apart. A roar louder than any mortal voice ripped through the valley, shaking the fortress, splintering stone and sky alike. The mountain woke. A great column of black smoke rose from its peak, twisting like a serpent from the underworld. The air burned, the heat suffocating, und unholy, as if the very breath of the gods had been unleashed upon the earth.

Then came the fire. Molten rock erupted from the crater, spilling like liquid death down the mountainside, consuming everything in its path, trees, fields, homes.

Xelhua, standing over the bleeding form of Izel, watched in horrified awe. He had wanted Turrialba. Now, he watched her burn, for the gods had accepted her sacrifice. Before their eyes, Turrialba's body was consumed by the fire, her silhouette vanishing in the raging glow of the inferno. As she was taken, her scream did not sound like pain. It sounded like vengeance.

By dawn, the valley was unrecognizable. The fortress was gone, swallowed by ash and ruin. The once-green forests lay in charred remains, with just blackened husks where life had once flourished. The volcano stood taller than before, its peak crowned with a wreath of smoke, as if it had crowned itself a king.

Of Turrialba, there was no trace. No grave, no ashes, only the eternal, unyielding mountain that bore her name and so the legend lives on. The valley never forgot. Some say, on nights when the moon is high, when the smoke from the volcano curls in the shape of a woman's silhouette, you can still hear her voice. It is a whisper upon the wind and a warning, a curse. The mountain still remembers the sacrifice that it was offered, and it still hungers for more.

Legend Of The Accursed Bell

This story has been adapted from a tale originally told by Thomas A. Janvier in Legends Of The City Of Mexico, published in 1910 by Harper & Brothers Publishers, New York. Legends of the City of Mexico delves into the rich cultural heritage of Mexico, exploring the myths and legends that have been passed down through generations. The book included a diverse range of stories, drawing from Aztec, Spanish, and indigenous Mexican traditions.

This story is about the cursed bell, the same bell that once served as the clock bell of the Palace There was a curse upon this bell, and that was why it was put on trial by the Inquisition, condemned to have its wicked tongue torn out, and banished from Spain to this land. In fact, it was not a single curse, but a combination of many. These curses, having existed separately in different places, were later unleashed all at once and fused into one terrible affliction. The origins of this dreadful curse can be traced to a Moor named Muslef, a man called Don Gil de Marcadante, a suit of devil-forged armour, and the release of all curses from a holy cross, where they had been imprisoned for centuries.

When this holy emblem was melted down and reforged, the metal from it was used to cast the bell, and thus, all these curses were bound together within it.

Muslef had a dark reputation and met a violent end. A Christian knight killed him in battle, severing his head as a trophy and taking great pride in his victory. But the knight also brought back Muslef's armour, a bronze suit, intricately and beautifully crafted, and so finely worked that it must have been forged by devils themselves. Worse still, it carried an evil presence, for it had been worn by an infidel. Had the knight sought the blessing of a priest to exorcise the evil spirits bound to it, the armour might have been purified. But he failed to do so. As a result, the devils remained trapped within, waiting for their chance to unleash chaos.

How Don Gil de Marcadante came into possession of this cursed armour, I do not know. Perhaps it was made for him, or perhaps he simply found that it fitted him well. What is certain is that he was as sinful as the curse itself. Don Gil was a law student in Toledo, but his studies were the least of his concerns. His shameful lifestyle was the scandal of the city, bringing disgrace upon his respectable brother and despair to his poor mother. He openly and habitually broke every commandment, flaunting his wickedness for all to see.

Hot-tempered and quick to violence, he was a born brawler, always ready to duel at the slightest provocation. When angered, he would curse so violently that his mouth seemed to spew serpents, toads, and scorpions. He never hesitated to draw his sword, and he moved from words to bloodshed in an instant. At his most good-natured, he was merely indifferent after murdering someone in a fight. But even in those rare moments, his temper remained frighteningly unpredictable. Few dared to associate with him.

It became clear that Don Gil had dealings with the devil himself. Many supernatural occurrences surrounded him. A wound he received in a duel healed instantly before the onlookers' eyes. On another occasion he was seen pulling apart thick iron bars from a window as though they were silk threads. He once threw a stone at a man in rage, and though it missed, it remained burning hot for days where it landed.

At night, in a hidden part of his house, he performed dark and blasphemous rituals, with Satan himself as his companion. The Holy Office of the Inquisition took notice. It was clear that Don Gil was a sorcerer, and so he was seized and imprisoned, still wearing the cursed armour, which by now had become even more tainted by his sins.

The Inquisition chained Don Gil securely in his prison cell, fastening him to a heavy iron ring embedded in the wall. He was to remain there until the next auto-da-fé, where he would burn at the stake as a proper and righteous punishment. But sometimes the devil looks after his own. One morning, when the jailer arrived with his usual ration of bread and water, he unlocked the door and saw, or thought he saw, Don Gil, standing there in his armour, waiting for his meal.

But then, a terrible realisation struck him. What he was looking at was not Don Gil at all. The armour stood upright, but it was completely empty. The chain had been broken. The iron ring had been torn from the wall. And Don Gil was gone.

Then, to the jailer's utter horror, the empty suit of armour began to move. It walked slowly across the cell, its hollow form clanking eerily with each step. Overcome with terror, the jailer lost his mind on the spot.

After that day, Don Gil was never seen or heard of again. When the time came for his execution at the auto-da-fé, he had to be burned in effigy, for his soul had already been taken by the devil. However, as there was no doubt about the place to which he had been taken, everyone was content knowing that he would receive his true punishment elsewhere.

It was then that the Holy Office wisely ordered that his cursed, devil-possessed armour be melted down and reforged into a cross. They believed that the sanctity of the cross would neutralise the evil curses and bind the devils within it. Some doubted the wisdom of using such unholy metal for a sacred emblem, but when the armour was thrown into the furnace, their doubts were quickly dispelled.

As the molten metal churned, the workmen recoiled in horror, for from within the flames, they heard shrieks of devilish laughter, blasphemies, and unearthly curses. When the metal was poured into the mould, the screams turned into howls of defiance, which gradually weakened as the metal solidified into a cross. The final sounds were agonised cries, then faint lamentations, and at last, only whimpering moans.

Thus, the devils and the curses were trapped within the cross, which was then erected in a small town near Madrid, where a cross had been needed at the time. For hundreds of years, it stood there undisturbed.

Over time, those who knew of the cross's dark secret passed away, and eventually, a Prior from a nearby convent requested it to be melted down and recast into a bell. His request was granted, as he was a good and pious man who genuinely needed a bell for his convent. Thus, the cursed metal was once again melted and reshaped, this time into a magnificent bell. It was adorned with a two-headed eagle on one side, a Calvary scene on the other, and two imperial lions supporting a crown-shaped crossbar at the top

When it was hung in the convent tower, the Prior and his brothers were delighted. But their joy did not last. Without warning, in the dead of night, the entire town was jolted awake by the furious ringing of the bell. Its violent clangs shattered the silence of the darkness, filling the air with deafening noise. The townsfolk, the Señor Cura, the Señor Alcalde, the alguaciles, the Prior, and all the monks rushed outside in terror. There, they discovered that the bell tower was locked, yet the bell was ringing on its own.

At first, only the Señor Alcalde, a brave and sceptical man, refused to believe it was the work of the devil. Determined to uncover the truth, he had the tower unlocked and entered with a torch in hand. Inside, he froze in horror. The bell rope flew wildly up and down, as if dozens of invisible hands were pulling it, yet there was no one there. His courage wavered, but he crossed himself and pressed on.

Climbing to the belfry, he was met with an even more chilling sight. The bell swung violently, tolling with tremendous force, yet no human touched it. The only living creature in the tower was a huge black cat, its fur bristling, its tail puffed out, and its green eyes gleaming in the torchlight. The demonic creature locked eyes with him, hissing wickedly, before leaping past him and vanishing into the night.

Now convinced that the devil himself was ringing the bell, the Señor Alcalde called down for the Señor Cura to take control of the situation. The priest climbed the stairs, holding his aspergillum filled with holy water.

The Consejo of the Inquisition then passed its final ruling, namely that the bell posed no threat to good Christians, that it was, however, possessed by demons, meaning that its tongue must be removed, so it could never ring again, and finally that since it was dangerous, it was to be banished from Spain and sent to the Indies. Thus, the bell was removed, its tongue was torn out, and it was shipped to Mexico, where it was abandoned in a palace corridor, untouched for years.

It remained there until over a century later, when the Conde de Revillagigedo became Viceroy of New Spain. Ever the pragmatist, he saw no reason for a perfectly good bell to sit idle. When he asked about it, he was told only that it was cursed. Unconvinced, he pressed further, until a very old clerk uncovered an ancient royal decree, confirming the bell's demonic history.

Even the bold Viceroy hesitated to defy such an order. But being a clever man, he realised that a clock bell, which is struck externally, did not require a tongue. Thus, he had the bell installed in the Palace clock, technically obeying the decree while making use of it once more.

For many years, the cursed bell rang regularly, perhaps because the demons inside had grown old, or because the curse had weakened with time. All was well until the French Intervention. When the French meddled with everything, they replaced the bell and had it melted down. Yet, even in its final moments, the curse refused to die.

A master founder once told the tale that when the bell was melted, the metal turned sour, becoming impossible to recast. If that is true, then it seems that, even after centuries of exile, the devils within the bell still had some wickedness left in them.

The Golden Voice of Poás

This story is my own adaptation of a traditional regional tale. This tale is based on Costa Rican sources.

The village of Alba Serena lay cradled in the emerald arms of the Poás Volcano, a place where mist curled lazily around ancient trees and the land pulsed with an unseen magic. This was a land where spirits whispered on the wind, where the mountains had secrets, and where Maria was born.

From the moment she could speak, Maria did not simply talk, she sang. Her voice was not of this world. It was a melody so pure, so hauntingly beautiful, that the breeze seemed to pause and listen. The birds hushed their songs, the river slowed its current, and even the trees leaned in as if enchanted.

She was the daughter of humble farmers, people who lived quietly, tilled the soil and spoke with reverence of the volcano, but Maria's voice was a gift that could not be contained. Word spread far beyond the village, and soon, strangers came from distant lands, drawn by the girl whose singing could make the stars tremble.

But magic always has a price, and there were those who listened with ears of envy rather than awe.

One twilight evening, as Maria sat by the crystal-clear river that ran from the slopes of Poás, she sang a song of longing, a song not meant for human ears.

The water stirred. The earth shivered beneath her bare feet. From the mist rising off the river, a shape took form, not a man, not a beast, but something older, something woven from smoke and ember, from stone and wind. The Guardian of Poás was neither kind nor cruel, neither man nor god, but something in between, a force bound to the volcano, watching, waiting, shaping the fate of the land. Its eyes, black as the depths of the earth, regarded Maria with solemn reverence.

"You are more than flesh, child," it murmured, its voice like the murmur of lava flowing beneath stone. "Your voice does not belong to mortals alone. It stirs the ancient powers of this land. I have watched. I have listened. And I would offer you a gift."

In its spectral hands, it held a necklace of gold, adorned with jewels that shimmered like captured firelight.

"Take this, Maria, and your voice shall rise beyond mortal limits. The mountains will echo your song, and even the spirits of the volcano shall weep at its beauty."

Maria, young and trusting, took the necklace and clasped it around her throat. The moment it touched her skin, a shudder passed through the earth, and Maria became something other than human.

The transformation was immediate. Maria's voice, already divine, became something otherworldly. When she sang, the rivers glowed, the winds carried her melody across valleys, and animals stood transfixed, bewitched by the sound. Her fame spread like wildfire, and soon, kings sent envoys to hear her song.

But with her rising fame came whispers in the dark. Jealousy curdled like poison in the hearts of men. Some said her power was unnatural, a thing to be feared and controlled. Others claimed she had bargained with demons, that she was no longer a girl, but a cursed spirit trapped in flesh.

One night, Maria returned home to find her father pale with fear. "You must flee, child," he whispered. "The people… they speak of you in nervous voices. They say no human should wield such power. There are those who would take it from you, by force if they must."

Maria's hands trembled. She had only ever sung for joy, to bring light into the world, and now, that light had drawn shadows to her doorstep. Desperate, she ran to the river, calling upon the one who had given her the gift. And once again, the Guardian of Poás appeared.

"They seek to silence you," it said, its voice filled with something that might have been pity, or amusement, or both. "The world fears what it cannot control."

Maria knelt before the spirit. "I only wish to sing. But I do not wish to be hunted for it."

The spirit regarded her in silence. Then, it lifted one hand, and in it formed a cloak of night itself, woven from mist and shadow. "Then take this, child. It will hide you from those who wish you harm. Wear it, and you shall walk unseen, heard only when you choose to be heard."

With a trembling hand, Maria took the Cloak of the Mist, wrapping herself in its embrace. And the world forgot her.

Maria vanished from mortal sight. Her name became a whisper, a legend spoken of in hushed, longing tones. Some claimed they still heard her in the valleys, her voice threading through the wind like a ghostly hymn. Others believed she had been taken by the volcano, swallowed by the Guardian who had once blessed her.

But Maria was not gone. She walked among the people unseen, hidden beneath the Cloak of the Mist, her voice a thing of rumour and wonder. Sometimes, when the night was still and the moon hung low over Poás, she would stand atop a ridge, and she would sing once more.

In the distance, from the heart of the volcano, came an answering voice, a deep, ancient hum that resonated through the stone, a reminder that the Guardian still listened.

Epilogue: The Eternal Song

The village of Alba Serena still exists. The volcano still looms, its smoke curling like silent prayers to forgotten gods. To this day, when the wind moves just right, a song drifts through the valleys, a song too pure, too sorrowful, and too haunting to belong to any living throat. The villagers bow their heads, listening in reverence, for they know that Maria still sings. She always will.

And the Guardian of Poás still watches over her, bound forever in the melody of the mountain.

Legend Of The Callejón Del Padre Lecuona

This story has been adapted from a tale originally told by Thomas A. Janvier in Legends Of The City Of Mexico, published in 1910 by Harper & Brothers Publishers, New York. Legends of the City of Mexico delves into the rich cultural heritage of Mexico, exploring the myths and legends that have been passed down through generations. The book included a diverse range of stories, drawing from Aztec, Spanish, and indigenous Mexican traditions.

Padre Lanchitas was truly loved, for he was a man of kindness and devotion. He cared for everyone, offering comfort to the sick and troubled, and giving his aid freely. To confess to him was not a burden, but a joy, and his absolution was worth having, for it was always given with God's blessing.

One dark and dreary night, rain fell heavily, and a chill wind blew through the streets. Padre Lanchitas hurried through the storm, eager to reach the house of a dear friend, where he was expected for his weekly game of malilla, a serious game, requiring a keen mind and great skill. He was running late, which is why he moved so quickly.

Just as he neared his friend's house, grateful to finally be out of the cold and wet, he felt a tug on his cloak. Turning, he saw an old woman, her face lined with desperation.

"For the love of God, Padre!" she pleaded. "Come quickly! A man is dying and he needs confession before it is too late!"

A priest cannot refuse such a call, but Padre Lanchitas hesitated. His absence would inconvenience his friends, for they could not play malilla without him. "Why have you not gone to the local parish priest?" he asked.

"Because," she insisted, "the dying man will only confess to you! Please, hurry! If you do not come, his soul will be lost, and when you face God yourself, you will bear the sin of refusing him!"

At this, Padre Lanchitas relented, following the woman through the dark, muddy streets as the rain continued to pour down.

At last, they arrived at the eastern end of Callejón del Padre Lecuona, stopping in front of a long, ancient house. It faced the Church of El Carmen, its high walls topped with a distinct hump. It was a very old house, built back when Mexico was ruled by Viceroys, long before the time of President Porfirio. The building had no windows, only a large carriage entrance at one end, a small door in the middle, and another small door at the far end. The old woman led him to the middle door. It was unlocked, and with a gentle push, she opened it, ushering him inside.

The moment he stepped in, Padre Lanchitas recoiled, for a foul stench filled the air. It was the stench of decay, the kind found in old, abandoned houses, where windows and doors have remained sealed for far too long. Clutching his handkerchief to his nose, he moved forward. There was little light, only a single candle, its weak flame flickering from a nail stuck into a wooden board in the far corner.

On the earth floor, a man lay on a mat, covered by a ragged, filthy blanket. The room was otherwise empty, except for thick cobwebs, deep shadows, the old woman, and the stench that clung to everything.

Approaching, Padre Lanchitas took the candle in his hand, stepping toward the motionless figure. He pulled back the blanket and stumbled back in horror.

"This man is already dead!" he gasped. "He cannot confess! And by the look of him, he has been dead for a long time!"

Beneath the candlelight, he saw a withered face, the skin yellowed and stretched tight over bone. The eyes were sunken and closed, and the hands, folded across the chest, were little more than dry skin clinging to skeletal fingers. A long-dead corpse lay before him.

At that moment, a terrible unease crept into the Padre's heart. The cold night, the darkened house, the pleading old woman, the dreadful stench…something was terribly wrong.

The woman looked at the priest with certainty but also with a gentle insistence. "Padrecito, this man is going to confess."

With that, she moved to the far corner of the room, retrieved the wooden board with a nail in it, took the candle from the priest's hand, and fixed it back onto the nail.

In the dim flickering light, the man on the mat sat up. His shadow stretched long and eerie across the wall, and in a voice that carried a dry, rasping tone, he began to recite the Confiteor Deo.

At that point, the priest had no choice but to listen. What the man confessed that night, being spoken under the seal of confession, remained a secret, but word spread later that he had spoken of events from over two hundred years ago. The priest, being well-read in history, recognised details from that ancient time. And what shocked him most was that the man placed himself at the heart of those events, describing a terrible crime that he had committed.

He ended his confession with a startling revelation. In that long-gone era, he had been killed in a brawl, struck down suddenly and left to die without confession or absolution. Because of this, his soul had been condemned to hell, suffering in eternal torment ever since.

Hearing such wild talk, the priest dismissed it as the fevered ramblings of a dying man. He told him to rest, promising that he would return to take his true confession once his delirium had passed.

But the man cried out desperately, "No, Father, it cannot wait! By God's mercy, I have been given one single chance to return from Eternity to confess my sins! If you do not hear me now, I will be lost forever, dragged back into the burning torment of hell!"

The priest was convinced now that the man was completely mad, but to calm him, he let him speak. The man unburdened his soul, confessing his horrifying sins in full. When he was done, the priest gave him absolution, not because he believed his tale, but to ease his suffering, much as one might promise the moon to a restless child.

Yet that night, the devil himself must have trembled, for the kindness of a good priest had cost him a soul that should have been his own.

As Padre Lanchitas spoke the final words of absolution, the man collapsed onto his mat. His body fell back with a dry, brittle sound, like the rattling of old bones. The candle burned low, its flame sputtering as though gasping for breath. The woman had vanished.

Feeling uneasy, the priest hurried outside, stepping into the darkened street. No sooner had he crossed the threshold than the door slammed shut behind him, as if unseen hands had forced it closed.

Outside, he expected to find the woman waiting for him, so he could tell her to call for him when the man's fever had broken, so he might take a true confession and offer real absolution. But she was nowhere to be seen.

Thinking that she must have slipped back inside, he knocked at the door, first lightly, then loudly. There was no answer. Trying the door, he pushed hard with all his strength. But it held firm, as if it were part of the stone wall itself.

Shaken, the priest made his way quickly to his friend's house, grateful to find warmth, light, and the company of living men.

He had walked so fast that when he removed his hat, his forehead was damp with sweat. Reaching into his pocket for his handkerchief, he found it was missing. This was no ordinary handkerchief, it was finely embroidered, with his initials woven into a wreath, a gift from a nun he had known in a convent where he had served as almoner. Not wishing to lose something so precious, he sent his friend's servant to the old house to retrieve it.

The servant returned a long time later, looking troubled. "The house is locked up tight, Father," he said. Then he added something even stranger: "A watchman saw me knocking and told me I was wasting my time. No one has lived in that house for years and years!"

The mystery deepened.

That night, Padre Lanchitas shared part of what had happened with his three trusted friends. By chance, one of them was a notary who managed the estate to which that house belonged. The notary swore that no one had lived there for decades. The house had been tied up in legal disputes, standing locked and empty for a lifetime. He was certain the priest had simply mistaken it for another house, given that everything had happened in the dark and rain.

But Padre Lanchitas was just as certain that he had made no mistake. They argued over it until they finally agreed that the next morning, they would go together to the house, and the notary would bring the key.

The next day, they met outside the house. The priest led them to the middle door, the one the old woman had opened so effortlessly. The notary pointed out something unsettling before unlocking it. The door was covered in cobwebs, undisturbed. The keyhole was clogged with years of dust, proof that no key had been used in generations. The other doors were the same. And yet…

When the notary finally forced the rusty lock open, they stepped inside. The house was dark and empty, nothing but bare walls and silence. But there was one thing. The priest smelled it instantly, a foul, rotten stench.

"All old houses smell like this," the notary said dismissively.

But Padre Lanchitas knew better. He was ready to leave when something caught his eye. Over in the far corner of the room, just beside where the dying man had lain, he saw something gleaming pale in the dim light. Bending down, he picked it up. It was his handkerchief.

That was proof enough for the notary. They left the dark, cursed house as quickly as they could, stepping into the blessed warmth of the sun. But Padre Lanchitas was forever changed.

He knew then the terrible truth that he had heard the confession of a dead man. Worse still, he had given absolution to a soul that had come burning hot from hell. From that day forward, he never wore his hat again. For the rest of his life, he walked bareheaded, a silent penance for the absolution he had given. He devoted himself entirely to the poor, his days filled with prayer, fasting, and charity. And when he finally died, it was said that within the walls of that old house, they found the bones of the dead.

El Sisimito

This story is my own adaptation of a traditional regional tale. This version of the tale was largely informed by sources from Belize.

Deep in the lush, untamed jungles of Central America, where howler monkeys held philosophical debates from the treetops and parrots gossiped about the latest jungle scandals, there lived a creature so peculiar, so utterly ridiculous, that nobody quite knew what to make of it. His name was El Sisimito.

Now, you might have heard terrifying stories about this beast, tales about how he lurked in the undergrowth, ready to pounce on unsuspecting villagers, but frankly, that was a load of jungle dung.

El Sisimito was no monster. He was a trickster. A prankster of the highest order. And, most importantly, he was a lover of riddles, puzzles, and general nonsense.

Covered in mossy green fur, with arms slightly too long and feet slightly too large, El Sisimito could blend into the jungle as easily as a chameleon wearing camouflage trousers. His greatest talent, however, was mimicry. He could imitate anything, be it the screech of a toucan, the creaking of ancient trees, or even the voice of the village chief demanding more tortillas at dinner time.

And oh, how he loved confusing people. It was harmless fun! A bit of jungle mischief! But humans, as it turned out, were incredibly easy to startle, a fact El Sisimito found endlessly amusing. But one day, he met a boy named Miguel, and everything changed.

Miguel was ten years old, which meant he was completely fearless and absolutely convinced he knew everything. One morning, a group of villagers set out into the jungle to collect medicinal plants, rare fruits, and anything else that wasn't nailed down. Among them was Miguel, determined to prove himself the bravest of them all.

But the jungle is no place for the overconfident. The deeper they ventured, the stranger things became. First, the trees began whispering. Then, the river laughed at them. And finally, a voice eerily similar to Miguel's grandmother called out from the undergrowth, saying, "Miguel! Did you remember to wash your hands before leaving the house?"

Miguel froze mid-step. The villagers exchanged terrified glances. Miguel's grandmother was three miles away, comfortably at home, drinking hot chocolate and muttering about how kids these days had no respect for proper hygiene.

The jungle fell silent. Then they heard a voice going "Hee hee hee!"

A high-pitched giggle echoed through the trees. The villagers, deciding that this was a perfect time to panic, began running in different directions, their baskets of herbs flung into the air. Miguel, now completely disoriented, stumbled headfirst into a large tree root and landed flat on his face.

As he pulled himself up, rubbing his nose, he realized he was alone. Well, not quite alone, for something was watching him.

Emerging from the twisting vines, grinning from ear to ear, was El Sisimito. "Oh-ho! What have we here? A little lost human? My, my, what a terrible predicament!"

Miguel gulped. The creature was short but strangely lanky, covered in shaggy moss-coloured fur, and had mischief written all over his face.

"You're El Sisimito!" Miguel blurted. "The jungle trickster!"

El Sisimito gave a dramatic bow. "Guilty as charged! And you, my dear human, are terribly lost. Oh, woe! Oh, tragedy! However shall you escape my domain?"

Miguel scowled. "You're the reason we got lost in the first place!"

El Sisimito feigned surprise. "Me? Surely you jest! I am merely a humble… well, actually, I am not humble at all. But I do love a good game!"

Miguel's mind raced. He remembered something his grandmother had once told him. El Sisimito loved riddles. So he took a deep breath, steadied himself, and declared, "I challenge you to a battle of wits!"

El Sisimito's eyes gleamed. "A challenge?" he purred. "Oh, I do love a challenge. Very well, little human! A riddle contest it shall be! If you win, I will guide you home. But if I win…"

He paused for dramatic effect.

"I shall turn you into a coconut!"

Miguel blinked. "You… can do that?"

El Sisimito shrugged. "Not really, but it adds to the suspense!"

And so, the Great Jungle Riddle-Off began.

They took turns, hurling riddles at each other like coconuts in a monkey fight.

"I have cities but no houses, I have mountains but no trees, I have water but no fish. What am I?" Miguel asked.

"A map!" El Sisimito grinned.

El Sisimito countered, "I speak without a mouth and hear without ears. I have no body, but I come alive with the wind. What am I?"

Miguel frowned, thinking hard. Then his face lit up. "An echo!"

For hours they went back and forth. Birds stopped to watch in fascination. A monkey took notes on a leaf. Even the trees leaned in, eager for the outcome. But Miguel was very clever.

Finally, El Sisimito stroked his chin. "Alright, human," he said. "One last riddle. If you solve it, you win."

He leaned in close.

"What has roots as nobody sees, is taller than trees, up, up it goes, and yet it never grows?"

Miguel's eyes widened. He looked around. He looked at the trees. He looked at the sky. Then, slowly, he turned to face the mighty Poás Volcano, rising above them. He smiled. "A mountain."

El Sisimito threw his hands in the air. "Gah! Foiled again!"

Then, with a theatrical sigh, he snapped his fingers.

A path opened through the trees, revealing the way home.

"You win, little human," El Sisimito said with a wink. "You have earned my respect! Now go before I change my mind and actually turn you into a coconut."

Miguel, grinning, dashed through the opening. Miguel made it back to the village, where he was hailed as a hero. To this day, travellers in the jungle still hear laughter in the trees, whispers of El Sisimito's tricks, and the occasional riddle carried on the wind.

And if you ever find yourself lost in the jungles of Central America, just remember, El Sisimito loves a challenge. And he's always looking for his next great riddle battle.

Legend Of The Living Spectre

This story has been adapted from a tale originally told by Thomas A. Janvier in Legends Of The City Of Mexico, published in 1910 by Harper & Brothers Publishers, New York. Legends of the City of Mexico delves into the rich cultural heritage of Mexico, exploring the myths and legends that have been passed down through generations. The book included a diverse range of stories, drawing from Aztec, Spanish, and indigenous Mexican traditions.

Ghostly apparitions of the dead are common enough. I myself have seen several spectres, as have many of my friends. But the spectre I am about to tell you of was unlike any other.

This was no spirit of a dead man. He was alive, wearing his own flesh and bones, walking and talking just like any other living person. Yet, despite this, there was no doubt that he was a ghostly figure, because at the exact same moment he was seen here in Mexico City, he was also seen thousands of miles away, in a completely different part of the world. Clearly, his journey could only have been made on the wings of the devil himself.

The exact date of this extraordinary event is well recorded. It happened the day after the Governor of the Philippines, Don Gómez Pérez Dasmariñas, was brutally murdered. That unfortunate gentleman had his skull split open and died in the Molucca Islands on the 25th of October 1593. Since we know this event was accurately documented, there can be no doubt that the story I am telling you is completely true.

On that very same day, as the great doors of the Palace in Mexico stood under guard, something utterly baffling took place. The sentries, along with passersby in the Plaza Mayor, suddenly noticed a soldier marching back and forth in front of the Palace gates. He patrolled his post just as any sentry would, marching with discipline, his musket on his shoulder, turning sharply, and even saluting officers as they passed. But there was something strange about him.

His expression was one of confusion, as if he were dazed and bewildered. And no one recognised him. His uniform was entirely unfamiliar, made from a different fabric and cut than those worn by any regiment stationed in Mexico. Then, one of the guards who had served in the Philippines realised what it was. This was the uniform of the Palace Guard in Manila.

The sentry was a man of about forty, strong and well-built, with the air of a seasoned soldier. Even in his confusion, he carried himself with confidence, as if he had faced many battles and could handle whatever fate threw his way. When questioned, he spoke with a boldness that suggested he was no stranger to adventure, even if it involved witches or demons.

It did not take long for the Captain of the Guard to be summoned. When he arrived, he demanded answers. "Who are you?" he asked sternly. "Where have you come from? And what do you think you're doing standing guard at a post where you were never assigned?"

The stranger answered, without hesitation and with complete confidence. "My name is Gil Pérez. I come from the Philippines. And I am simply doing my duty as best I can." He glanced around, confused but resolute. "This may not be the Governor's Palace where I was posted this morning, but it is a governor's palace, and so I am doing my best to fulfil my orders."

Then, quite casually, as if discussing an everyday event, he added, "Oh, and by the way, Governor Don Gómez Pérez Dasmariñas was assassinated last night in the Molucca Islands. His head was split open and he died from the wound."

This strange sentry had already appeared out of nowhere, wearing a foreign uniform, and now he was claiming that the Governor of the Philippines had been murdered the night before, on an island in the Pacific Ocean, thousands of miles away! Such a serious matter had to be investigated by the Viceroy himself. And so, Gil Pérez was immediately taken before Don Luis de Velasco, the Viceroy of New Spain at the time.

Even before such a powerful man, Gil Pérez remained calm and composed. He repeated his story exactly as he had told it before, with the same cool manner, using the same words, and showing not the slightest sign of fear or hesitation. Naturally, the Viceroy questioned him sharply, attempting to catch him out. But whether he was giving answers or admitting he had none, Gil Pérez stood firm. He had the confidence of a soldier, a man who had spent years facing danger and would not allow his word to be doubted, even by a Viceroy.

And should anyone of lesser rank challenge him? Well, he seemed quite prepared to defend himself with his fists or his sword.

If Gil Pérez was telling the truth, then the only explanation was impossible. He had somehow travelled across the world in an instant, appearing in Mexico City at the very moment he had last been seen standing guard in Manila. Had he been transported by witchcraft? A divine miracle? Or had the devil himself carried him on unseen wings?

What is certain is that this case left the entire city bewildered. And to this day, the mystery of Gil Pérez remains one of the most extraordinary tales in history.

For the most part, Gil Pérez's explanation of his situation was clear and reasonable. The information he shared about his regiment was known to be accurate, as was much of what he described about events in the Philippines, which matched the latest news brought by the most recent galleon.

However, when it came to the real mystery, of how he had suddenly and inexplicably travelled across the vast ocean and the Earth itself, in a single instant, from his guard post in front of the Governor's Palace in Manila to the Viceroy's Palace in Mexico City, he had no explanation at all. He admitted that he did not know how it had happened, only that it had happened. He insisted that just half an hour earlier, he had been in Manila, and now he was undeniably in Mexico City, something the Viceroy himself could plainly see with his own eyes.

As for the even greater mystery of how he knew that, just the night before, the Governor of the Philippines had been brutally murdered in the Molucca Islands, he was just as bewildered. He could not explain how he knew it, only that he was certain it was true. He boldly stated that, in time, the news would arrive in Mexico through normal means, proving that everything he had said was accurate.

And so, having answered all of the Viceroy's questions, Gil Pérez simply stood there, completely at ease, his feet firmly planted, one hand resting on his hip, his arm akimbo, calmly waiting to hear what would happen next.

There was only one thing everyone could agree on. This was surely the work of the devil. There was also good reason to suspect that Gil Pérez himself was in much closer contact with the devil than any Christian man should be, even for an old soldier, from whom no great religious devotion was expected.

Wanting nothing more to do with this baffling affair, the Viceroy decided to hand it over to the Holy Office, who specialised in such matters. Gil Pérez was swiftly arrested and sent to Santo Domingo, where he was locked in one of the strongest cells of the Inquisition.

For most men, falling into the hands of the Inquisition would have been a fate worse than death, a cause for paralysing terror. But Gil Pérez was not most men. Being an old campaigner, he took it all in his stride and showed no fear whatsoever. He cheerfully remarked that, in his years of soldiering, he had found himself in far worse situations.

And, in fact, he rather enjoyed his time in his cell. With a solid roof over his head, decent rations, and no need to march or fight, he considered himself more comfortable than any old soldier had a right to expect. His behaviour with the Inquisitors was also exemplary. He steadfastly maintained that, while the devil may have interfered with him, he himself had never had dealings with the devil.

He seemed to genuinely enjoy confessing as many of his sins as he could conveniently remember, and he conducted himself as a good Christian, at least as much as could be expected from a man of his background.

Meanwhile, the Inquisitors were left completely baffled. They debated endlessly about what they should do with him, but the problem remained the same. Had the devil used Gil Pérez for his own purposes? That seemed clear. But had Gil Pérez willingly made a pact with the devil? That was far less certain.

It hardly seemed fair to burn him at the stake when he himself insisted that he was just as much a victim as anyone else. So, while the Inquisitors remained locked in debate, Gil Pérez remained quite content, enjoying his leisurely life in Santo Domingo. And so, the months passed.

Then, one day, a galleon from the Philippines arrived at Acapulco, carrying proof that everything Gil Pérez had said was true. The ship brought confirmation that the Governor of the Philippines, Don Gómez Pérez Dasmariñas, had indeed been murdered. His crew had mutinied and split his skull open, exactly as Gil Pérez had described, and at precisely the time he had stated.

To make matters even stranger, one of the military officers who had arrived on the galleon immediately recognised Gil Pérez upon seeing him in Mexico City. This officer swore that he had seen him on duty in Manila, standing guard at the palace, only a day or two before the galleon's departure. With this final piece of evidence, there was no longer any doubt. Gil Pérez had somehow been transported from Manila to Mexico in an instant. And, since no human power could have accomplished this, it was clear that only the devil could have been responsible. Thus, by incontrovertible logic, the Holy Office concluded that Gil Pérez had been in league with the devil.

For one final time, the Inquisitors gathered to discuss the matter. After much deliberation, they reached a somewhat contradictory verdict: Gil Pérez was innocent, but he had definitely consorted with the devil. Therefore, he was to be released from his cell. However, as a dangerous and corrupting influence, he was to be sent back to Manila on the next galleon. And so, that was their final ruling.

As expected, Gil Pérez took the news in stride. His only complaint, which, for an old soldier, was entirely understandable, was that he had to leave his comfortable life of leisure and return to marching, guarding, and fighting once more. Thus, he was sent back to the Philippines, but this time in the ordinary manner, aboard a galleon, rather than on the devil's wings.

To my mind, though, there are still parts of this story left untold. For one, I cannot understand why the Holy Office, despite being convinced that the devil had transported him across the world, chose to be so lenient. And, even more mysteriously, what happened to Gil Pérez when he returned to Manila? Surely, after being absent from duty for half a year, he would have had some explaining to do.

Did he dare tell his superiors that he had been abducted by the devil himself? That is something I have never heard mentioned. And so, what I have told you is all that remains of this strange tale.

El Silbón

This story is my own adaptation of a traditional regional tale. This version of the tale was largely informed by sources from Venezuela.

The plains of Venezuela stretched wide and endless, a land of golden grass and restless winds, where the nights were vast and star filled, and whispers of the past clung to the air like mist. It was a land of legends, and among them, none was more feared than the tale of El Silbón, The Whistler.

But before he was a curse, he was a man.

His name was Silvano, the son of Don Elías, a rancher wealthy in land but poor in patience. Don Elías was a man of discipline, forged by the hardships of the land, and he expected his son to follow his path.

But Silvano was not like his father. He was lazy, spoiled, and arrogant, with an appetite for drink and vice that shamed the family name. He ignored his duties, mocked the ranch hands, and spent his nights staggering home reeking of liquor, leaving behind unpaid debts and broken promises.

"You disgrace our name!" Don Elías roared one evening, as Silvano stumbled into the ranch house, too drunk to stand properly. "You waste your life like a pig in the mud, bringing ruin to this family!"

Silvano laughed bitterly, eyes glazed with rage and intoxication. "You're just an old man, rotting on your land," he slurred. "One day, this place will be mine, and there will be no more work, no more rules, only freedom!"

Don Elías' face twisted with fury. He struck his son across the face, sending him crashing to the floor like a broken doll. Silvano lay there for a moment, his pride shattered, his rage rising like bile. And that was when the darkness entered his soul.

Silvano did not sleep that night. As the house fell silent, he wandered deep into the plains, his heart pounding with hatred. His father would pay for his humiliation. Drunken, half-mad with wrath, he cursed into the wind, calling on the foulest creatures that lurked in the shadows just beyond human sight.

"Help me," he murmured to those shadows. "Give me the power to destroy him."

The air grew cold. The rustling grass ceased to move, as though the land held its breath. And then an inhuman presence emerged from the darkness. Its form was shifting, its eyes holes into a dark void, and its voice a chorus of scratches speaking as one.

"You wish for vengeance?" it asked, a sound that crawled into Silvano's skull like a thousand writhing worms.

Silvano nodded, trembling.

"Then you shall have it," the entity breathed. "But all things have a price."

It reached forward, touching Silvano's lips with cold, clawed fingers. Pain exploded in his chest. His throat burned, as though his voice was being ripped from his body.

"You shall be a herald of death," the creature promised. "Your song shall be that of despair. The world will fear you, and you shall roam forever. This is the price of your hatred."

And in that moment, Silvano ceased to be a man. He had become a cursed and vengeful wraith.

At dawn, Don Elías awoke to a silence more unnatural than death itself. Stepping onto the porch, he saw his ranch hands huddled together, as pale as ghosts.

"Señor," one of them stammered, pointing toward the trees. "It's… it's him."

Don Elías turned to look and his blood turned to ice. There, standing motionless in the mist, was Silvano. His clothes hung from his emaciated body in tatters. His eyes were hollow pits of blackness, his skin stretched thin and lifeless. Over his shoulder, he carried a large, bloodstained sack.

Then the whistling began, but it was no ordinary tune. It was a sound from the abyss, a haunting melody that rose and fell in eerie, unnatural tones, carrying the promise of death.

Don Elías staggered backward, his knees buckling. As he fell to his death, his heart stopping in mid beat, he knew this was no longer his son. This was El Silbón. The Whistler.

From that day, the Whistler roamed the plains, cursed to wander the endless dark, his presence marked by his haunting, bone-chilling tune. His prey were those who had betrayed their fathers, the ungrateful sons who dared to defy the blood that bore them. To hear his whistle close was a blessing, for it meant he had passed you by. But to hear it far away, that was a death sentence. For the Whistler's song was not bound by distance. If his eerie melody drifted from afar, it meant he was already near, watching, waiting. And when he came for you, there was no escape.

His sack, slung over his shoulder, was filled with the bones of his victims, and each new soul he claimed was added to his gruesome collection. Some say he still searches for his father, for the vengeance that was stolen from him. Others believe he is no longer man, nor even ghost, but a force of malevolence that will never die.

But all agree on one thing. If you hear a distant whistle on a windless night, run. Run, and do not look back, for El Silbón is always watching, and if he chooses you, you will never be seen again.

Legend Of The Calle De La Machincuepa

This story has been adapted from a tale originally told by Thomas A. Janvier in Legends Of The City Of Mexico, published in 1910 by Harper & Brothers Publishers, New York. Legends of the City of Mexico delves into the rich cultural heritage of Mexico, exploring the myths and legends that have been passed down through generations. The book included a diverse range of stories, drawing from Aztec, Spanish, and indigenous Mexican traditions.

The scandal that gave Calle de la Machincuepa its name caused a great uproar across the city. Every tongue in Mexico was buzzing with gossip, with most people blaming the young lady for committing such a public and shameful act, even if it was done in pursuit of great wealth.

Some, however, argued that her uncle, the Marqués, was even more at fault for imposing such a bizarre and humiliating condition on his will. Others even placed the greatest blame on the Viceroy, for allowing such an improper spectacle to take place right in front of his palace, beneath his very nose.

As for me, I believe the young lady was the most culpable of all, for she had the freedom to choose, and she chose riches over dignity. This only confirmed what was already known, that she had a cold and selfish heart.

The Viceroy at the time was the Duque de Linares, who took office in 1714, so you can see that this strange event took place nearly three hundred years ago. At that time, there lived in what is now Calle de la Machincuepa a wealthy and noble Spanish gentleman named Don Mendo Quiroga y Suárez, known by his title, Marqués del Valle Salado.

However, Don Mendo had not been born noble, nor even of good lineage. His origins were unknown, and in his youth, he had sailed from Spain as a common sailor, seeking fortune on the sea. What exactly he did during those years remained a mystery, as he never spoke of it. However, it was widely believed that while he and his ship officially engaged in the slave trade, their true business was piracy. In fact, it was said that his fortune was built on blood and plunder.

After amassing a ship's worth of wealth, Don Mendo retired from his violent trade, arriving in Mexico to start a new life. With his illicit riches, he purchased the Valle Salado estate, where he established lucrative saltworks. Thanks to bribes and political influence, his wealth grew beyond measure. It was known for certain that he possessed a fortune of three and a half million pesos, a sum so vast that a hundred men could not finish counting it in an entire month. His extravagant gifts to the King of Spain earned him a noble title, and so, the former corsair became the Marqués del Valle Salado.

With his new status, Don Mendo lived in magnificent style, indulging in a lavish and scandalous lifestyle. Yet, despite his notorious past, he was respected by society and beloved by the poor for his charitable donations.

As old age crept upon him, Don Mendo began to suffer from the ailments brought on by his indulgent life. In his loneliness, he realised he had no wife and no children to care for him.

Around this time, his brother in Spain passed away, leaving behind a daughter. Seeing an opportunity, Don Mendo summoned his orphaned niece, Doña Paz de Quiroga, to Mexico, making her the head of his household and entrusting her with his care. In return, he lavished upon her every imaginable luxury.

Doña Paz was stunningly beautiful, and her exquisite clothing and glittering jewels only enhanced her elegance. Being named the sole heiress of her uncle's fortune and noble title, she soon became the most sought-after lady at the Viceroy's court. She was fiercely proud, ambitious, and had an unyielding sense of self-importance. Every young nobleman in Mexico City fell in love with her, while even the most respected clergymen and greatest aristocrats treated her with reverence. Even in her own home, she never let her guard down, conducting herself with an air of regal dignity. In public, she carried herself with such grandeur and poise that she might have been mistaken for a queen. However, despite all her charm, Doña Paz had a cold heart.

Though she owed everything to her uncle, Doña Paz treated Don Mendo with complete indifference. Instead of caring for him, she left him entirely in the hands of servants. When she did visit his sickbed, she would bring a perfumed handkerchief to cover her nose, complaining that the smell of balms and medicines was unbearable. She never once spoke a kind word to him, nor offered him a gentle glance. Naturally, Don Mendo resented her cruelty. And so, in secret, he made up his mind. One day, she would pay for her ingratitude.

When Don Mendo finally passed away, his will was read. At first, Doña Paz was delighted, the will repeatedly referred to her as his "beloved niece" and stated, in clear and undeniable terms, that every single peso of his vast fortune was hers. But then, at the very end of the will, a condition was revealed. Before she could inherit even a single coin, she had to fulfil one specific task. And that condition, was so outrageous, so humiliating, that Doña Paz nearly fainted with shock and shame.

Don Mendo had written the following at the very end of his will: "To my beloved niece, Paz, I leave my entire fortune, but only on the condition that she fulfils precisely the requirement I now set before her. This condition is as follows: She must dress in her finest ball gown and adorn herself with her most magnificent jewels. Then, in an open carriage, she must ride to the Plaza Mayor at noon. Once there, she must walk to the very centre of the square, bow her head to the ground, and, while still bowing, perform what the common people of Mexico call a 'machincuepa.'*

"Should my beloved niece, Paz, fail to meet this requirement within six months of my passing, my entire fortune shall instead be divided equally between the Convent of Nuestra Señora de la Merced and the Convent of San Francisco. My niece shall receive nothing. And I impose this condition upon her so that, in suffering the bitterness of public humiliation, she may taste just a fraction of the bitterness her cruelties have brought upon me in my final years."

You can imagine the horror of this proud and dignified young lady when she learned the terms of her inheritance! She found herself utterly unable to decide. On one hand, she thought, "It will be over in a moment, and then I shall be unimaginably rich, a marquessa in my own right, the wealthiest and most powerful lady in all of New Spain!"

But on the other hand, she told herself, "Precisely because of my great wealth and title, I shall be mocked even more viciously for degrading myself in such a scandalous act. If I go through with it, I will never escape the shame. I shall be known forever as the Marquessa de la Machincuepa!"

And so, day after day, she agonised, unable to make up her mind.

Meanwhile, as time slipped away, the Mercedarians and the Franciscans grew ever more confident that they would soon inherit Don Mendo's fortune. They spoke gleefully of new altars for their churches, of improvements to their convents, rubbing their hands together in eager anticipation.

Then came the very last day of the six-month deadline. The morning passed, and still, there was no sign of Doña Paz. Crowds gathered in the Plaza Mayor, whispering excitedly, watching and waiting. The Mercedarians and Franciscans beamed with satisfaction, now absolutely certain that the fortune was theirs. Then, just as the Palace clock struck half past eleven, the great doors of Don Mendo's house swung open.

An open carriage emerged. Inside sat Doña Paz, dressed in her most extravagant ball gown, adorned with dazzling jewels. Her face was ashen pale, like a corpse, but her hands did not tremble. Through the crowded streets, she rode, her carriage cutting through the throng like a funeral procession, until she reached the Plaza Mayor.

The crowd fell silent as she stepped out of the carriage. The people parted before her as she walked slowly to the centre of the square, where her servants had laid out a rich carpet for her. And then, as the

Palace clock struck noon, she bowed her head to the ground. Then, still bowing, she performed a machincuepa. Thus, Doña Paz secured her inheritance, but at the terrible cost of the humiliation Don Mendo had intended for her.

What became of her after that, I have never heard. Did she live in wealth and power? Did she withdraw from society, too ashamed to enjoy her riches? No one can say.

But one thing is certain: the street where she lived immediately became known as the Calle de la Machincuepa, and the fact that it still bears that name today proves that every word of this story is true.

The Meaning of a Machincuepa

In proper Spanish, it translates to "salto mortal", or "somersault", but in truth, it means much more than that. For it was not just a simple tumble that Doña Paz performed that day. He wanted her to perform an excessive, dramatic, almost acrobatic flip, right there, at high noon, in the middle of a packed Plaza Mayor. And that is how one of the proudest and most dignified women in New Spain became the Marquessa de la Machincuepa!

La Ciguapa

This story is my own adaptation of a traditional regional tale. This version of the tale was largely informed by sources from Venezuela and The Dominican Republic.

The jungle felt alive. The trees stretched like cathedral spires, their tangled branches weaving a canopy so thick that the sun barely kissed the damp, leaf-strewn floor. The air was thick with the scent of earth and decay, with the soft sounds of unseen creatures, punctuated by the occasional shriek of some night-stalking thing that did not fear the dark. No man should walk alone in these woods. And yet, Manuel did.

He had always been a restless soul, craving the untamed, seeking the thrill of the unknown. The village was too small for him, its rhythms too predictable. He had heard the tales of spirits and shadows, of the woman who lived between the trees, whose voice called men to ruin.

He had laughed when the old women warned him. He had mocked the men who whispered of her in fearful tones. "She is nothing but a story," he had scoffed. "A phantom made up to keep children from straying too far."

But now, standing alone beneath the great ribs of the jungle, he was not so sure. Somewhere, just beyond his sight, a woman laughed. It was a sound too light, too musical, like the chime of wind through bones. Manuel's breath caught in his throat. He turned, his heart drumming against his ribs. Then he saw her.

The moon had broken through the trees, silver light spilling into a clearing where she stood. She was beyond beauty, beyond mortal words. Her long, dark hair tumbled past her waist, nearly reaching the earth, its strands glistening like black river water. Her skin was the colour of rich, wet soil, and her eyes were deep and endless, like pools that led to another world.

She watched him, and Manuel forgot himself. He forgot his village. He forgot his name. He forgot that he had ever been anything before this moment.

Her lips curled into a smile, small and mischievous, a beckoning thing. He took a step forward, entranced, not noticing how his own sense of the world had gone so silent. He didn't see how his own shadow had lengthened, stretching unnaturally in her presence. But then, as got closer to her he did notice that, where she stood, there were no footprints in the damp earth. He looked at her feet. They were wrong. They were turned backward, so that if she walked away from him, her prints would lead toward him instead. It had to be a trick of the jungle, a trick of the mind.

Manuel tried to move away, tried to force his body to run, to scream, to break the spell that had woven around him like vines, but La Ciguapa tilted her head, and the world tilted with her.

"Come closer," she whispered.

And Manuel did.

He did not remember when she disappeared. One moment, she was there, her scent all around him, her fingers trailing ghost-like through the air. And then…nothing. He was alone in the clearing. Alone with her echoing laughter ringing in his mind. Manuel stumbled backward, his heart hammering, his throat suddenly dry as dust. He turned and ran.

The trees seemed to close in around him, the branches snatching at his clothes. The jungle floor snarled his steps, roots gripping his ankles like fingers. He gasped, fighting his way back toward the path, back toward home, toward safety, toward light. But even as he ran, he knew that he would never be free again.

Eventually Manuel struggled back to his village, but in truth Manuel was not truly there. He no longer slept. When he closed his eyes, he saw her face, her smile, her backward footprints leading him into the trees again. He no longer ate. Food turned to dust in his mouth, tasteless, weightless. He no longer spoke, for in his inner world there was no need for words. All that he could hear, all that consumed him was her laughter, ringing in his ears, calling him back to the jungle.

"Come closer," she whispered.

He sat on the edge of his cot, his eyes hollow, his body wasting away. His mother wept. His father prayed. The village healer burned sage and whispered blessings, trying to cast out whatever curse had taken root inside him. But Manuel did not care. For him, the village was no longer real. Only she was real.

One evening, as the moon swelled full in the sky, Manuel rose from his cot. The village was asleep, unaware that one of its own was about to pass over. He walked into the jungle, his bare feet silent against the damp earth. Somewhere, deep in the trees, she was waiting. Her laughter drifted through the night, soft as a sigh.

"Come closer," she whispered.

Manuel obeyed. He did not stop. Not even when the earth grew soft beneath him, swallowing his footsteps. Not even when the vines curled around his ankles, pulling him deeper into the heart of the wild. Not even when the trees sealed behind him, erasing his path, leaving nothing but silence.

By the time the sun rose again, Manuel was gone. His mother searched for him. His father cried his name. The village whispered of what they already knew.

"He saw her," they said, shaking their heads. "And now he belongs to her."

No body was ever found. But there was always the sound of laughter on the wind, weaving through the trees.

And footprints in the dirt that always led the wrong way.

Legend Of La Llorona

This story has been adapted from a tale originally told by Thomas A. Janvier in Legends Of The City Of Mexico, published in 1910 by Harper & Brothers Publishers, New York. Legends of the City of Mexico delves into the rich cultural heritage of Mexico, exploring the myths and legends that have been passed down through generations. The book included a diverse range of stories, drawing from Aztec, Spanish, and indigenous Mexican traditions.

As everyone knows, many strange and terrible things lurk in the City's streets at night, but none is as terrifying as La Llorona, the Wailing Woman.

She is far worse than the Fiery Cow, that blazing beast which gallops through the streets at midnight, breathing smoke, sparks, and flames. The Fiery Cow, while terrifying to behold, does no real harm. But La Llorona is as dangerous as she is feared.

At times, she appears as a quiet, respectable woman, wandering the streets in a white petticoat and a white reboso draped over her head. She might seem ordinary, until she suddenly begins to run, shrieking for her lost children. Anyone who dares speak to her meets instant death.

No one knows exactly when La Llorona's story began, nor where she came from. But what is certain is that, when she was alive, she committed terrible sins. Each time she bore a child, she would cast it into the canals surrounding the city, drowning it. She had many children, and for years she continued this horrific practice.

Eventually, her conscience tormented her, though whether it was a priest's warning or a divine message from the saints, no one can say. But from that moment on, she began wandering the streets in darkness, weeping and wailing.

Before long, people began to whisper of a woman who roamed the city at night, crying out in anguish. Many brave souls ventured out at midnight, hoping to see her, but she could only be seen when the streets were deserted, when she was truly alone.

At times, she would approach a sleeping watchman, waking him with a soft voice, asking, "What time is it?"

When he opened his eyes, he would see a woman dressed in white, her reboso covering her face. The watchman would answer, "It is midnight."

To which she would reply, "At twelve hours of this day, I must be in Guadalajara." Or perhaps San Luis Potosí, or another distant city, and then, with a heart-wrenching shriek, she would cry, "Where shall I find my children?"

And in an instant, she would vanish completely.

The watchman would be left frozen in terror, his senses shattered, feeling as though he had died. This happened many times, and many watchmen reported it to their officers, but their superiors refused to believe them. That is, until one night, when an officer of the watch encountered La Llorona himself.

Walking through the lonely street beside the Church of Santa Anita, the officer spotted a woman dressed in white. Thinking she was a beautiful young lady, he began to flirt with her. He urged her on, saying: "Take off your reboso, so I may see your lovely face."

Without hesitation, she removed her veil, and what he saw was not a face at all, but a bare grinning skull, attached to the bony remains of a skeleton. As he stood frozen in horror, she exhaled an icy breath, so cold that it froze his very blood. He collapsed to the ground in a deathly faint.

When he finally regained his senses, he was so shaken that he stumbled back to the Diputación, trembling, and told them everything. But before long, his life drained away, and he died from fright.

What is most terrifying about La Llorona is that she can be seen in multiple places at once. One person will spot her crossing the atrium of the Cathedral, while another will see her at the Arcos de San Cosme, and yet another at Salto del Agua, near the prison of Belén. Even more unbelievable, in a single night, she has been seen in Monterrey, Oaxaca, and Acapulco, great distances apart, and whoever speaks to her dies instantly.

It is not just in the city where she is seen. Travellers on lonely roads have also encountered her. Once, a group of men saw her walking alone and asked, "Where are you going on this deserted road?"

She turned to them, crying, "Where shall I find my children?"

And with a chilling scream, she disappeared into the night.

One of the travellers lost his mind from the shock. When they reached the city and told their tale, they were warned that many others had suffered the same fate.

Because so many fear her very few dare to speak to her anymore, which means fewer people die from her curse. Yet her piercing cries and the sound of her running footsteps are still heard, especially on stormy nights.

Martina the Beautiful Cockroach

This story is my own adaptation of a traditional regional tale. This version of the tale was largely informed by sources from Cuba.

In the bustling streets of old Havana, there lived a beautiful young cockroach named Martina. With her delicate antennae and graceful legs, Martina was the envy of all the insects in the neighbourhood. But despite her beauty, Martina's heart longed for true love.

Determined to find her perfect match, Martina sought the advice of her wise old grandmother. "Abuela," she asked, "how will I ever know if a suitor truly loves me for who I am?"

Abuela smiled knowingly and handed Martina a secret family recipe. "My dear," she said, "take this magic coffee bean and use it to test the intentions of your suitors. Only the one who proves himself worthy shall win your heart."

Armed with her grandmother's wisdom, Martina set out to find her true love. Suitors of all shapes and sizes came calling, from the handsome cricket with his charming serenades to the suave centipede with his smooth dance moves. But none of them seemed to capture Martina's heart.

Then one day, a dapper young rooster named Pérez strutted into Martina's life. With his colourful feathers and confident demeanour, Pérez seemed like the perfect match. But Martina was cautious, for she knew that true love was more than skin deep.

To put Pérez to the test, Martina brewed a pot of her grandmother's magic coffee and invited him over for a cup. As they sipped their drinks, Martina watched carefully for any signs of deception.

To Martina's surprise, Pérez didn't flinch when he tasted the bitter brew. Instead, he smiled warmly and declared, "Martina, mi amor, even if your coffee were as bitter as gall, I would still drink it gladly, for it is not the flavour of the coffee that matters, but the company in which it is shared."

Touched by Pérez's sincerity, Martina knew that she had found her true love. They danced together under the moonlit sky, their hearts overflowing with joy. From that day on, Martina and Pérez lived happily ever after, proving that love knows no boundaries and that beauty is found in the depths of the heart.

And as the years passed, Martina shared her grandmother's wisdom with future generations, teaching them to cherish love and to look beyond appearances, just as she had done. And so, the tale of Martina the Beautiful Cockroach became a beloved story in Cuban folklore, reminding all who heard it of the power of love and the beauty of acceptance.

Popol Vuh – Editor's Note

I have included the various books extant of Popol Vuh in the next pages as they represent a cohesive whole and are best read together. The Popol Vuh is one of the most important texts in Mesoamerican history and mythology, particularly for understanding the beliefs, traditions, and worldview of the K'iche' Maya civilization. For me, here's why it holds such significance:

The Popol Vuh is often referred to as the "Book of the Community" or the Maya Bible because it contains the creation myths, religious beliefs, and ancestral stories of the K'iche' Maya, a major Maya group in present-day Guatemala. It provides insight into their spiritual worldview, gods, and cosmology.

The text explains the origins of the world, the first humans, and the conflicts between gods and mortals. The Hero Twins, Hunahpu and Xbalanque, serve as central figures, undergoing trials in the underworld (Xibalba) and eventually transforming into the sun and moon. These myths mirror broader Maya beliefs about the cycle of life, death, and rebirth.

Beyond mythology, the Popol Vuh contains valuable information about the K'iche' political structure, moral values, and traditions. It describes their rituals, ceremonies, and respect for ancestors, offering historians and anthropologists a rare glimpse into Maya life before Spanish colonization.

The text was originally passed down orally for generations and was written in the K'iche' language using Latin script in the 16th century, after the Spanish conquest. This makes it one of the few surviving indigenous-written records of Maya culture, helping to preserve their heritage despite colonial suppression.

The Popol Vuh remains a crucial primary source for scholars studying Mesoamerican religions, mythology, and history. It helps connect Maya beliefs with those of the Aztecs, Olmecs, and other cultures, revealing common themes in the region's mythology.

Apart from its historical and religious significance, the Popol Vuh is also considered a masterpiece of indigenous literature. Its poetic structure, dramatic storytelling, and deep philosophical themes about humanity, destiny, and divine justice make it a remarkable work of world literature.

For the modern Maya people, the Popol Vuh remains a symbol of cultural identity and resilience. It has been studied, translated, and revived as part of efforts to reclaim indigenous history and traditions in Guatemala and beyond.

The Popol Vuh is a spiritual, historical, and cultural cornerstone of the Maya civilization, offering a unique perspective on one of the world's most sophisticated ancient societies. Its preservation allows modern generations to understand and appreciate the depth of Maya wisdom, storytelling, and cosmology.

Popol Vuh – Book 1

This story (along with the following story) has been adapted from a tale originally told by Lewis Spence in The Popol Vuh - The Mythic And Heroic Sagas Of The Kichés Of Central America, published in 1908 by David Nutt, London. The Popol Vuh is often regarded as the Mayan equivalent of the Bible, containing mythological narratives, creation stories, and accounts of the origins of the world and humanity according to Mayan cosmology. It was originally written in the K'iche' language, a Mayan language spoken by the K'iche' people of Guatemala, and later transcribed into Latin script by Spanish colonizers in the 16th century.

In the beginning, the universe was cloaked in darkness, and the mighty god Hurakan, the divine wind, moved through the void. With a single command, he brought the earth into existence.

The great gods gathered, Hurakan, Gucumatz, the serpent adorned with green feathers, and Xpiyacoc and Xmucane, the revered mother and father deities, to shape the world. They created animals, yet no humans walked the earth. To fill this absence, they carved small figures from wood, shaping the first people.

But these beings were flawed, soulless, ungrateful, and without devotion. They did not honour the gods, nor did they respect creation. Angered by their disobedience, the gods resolved to wipe them from existence.

At Hurakan's command, the Heart of Heaven unleashed a mighty flood, drowning the wooden people beneath surging waters. From the heavens, fiery resin rained down, consuming what remained.

Then, the beasts of the world turned against them. The bird Xecotcovach plucked out their eyes; Camulatz severed their heads; Cotzbalam devoured their flesh, and Tecumbalam crushed their bones to dust.

Because they had failed to honour Hurakan, the gods cast the world into darkness, and an unceasing storm raged. Even inanimate objects took vengeance. The very tools they had mistreated rose against them. Dogs and hens, once subservient, now bit their former masters. Millstones, worn from years of grinding, ground human flesh in return. Cups and dishes, scalded by hot food, now burned those who held them.

Terrified, the surviving wooden people fled, seeking refuge in their homes, trees, and caves. But the earth rejected them, and nowhere was safe. One by one, they were destroyed, their existence wiped from the world.

It is said that their descendants still live, their punishment incomplete. They became the little monkeys that swing through the forests, forever echoing the fate of a race doomed to fall.

Popol Vuh – The Myth Of Vukub-Cakix

This story echoes stories told in the creation myths of Mexico that appear earlier in this book.

In the aftermath of a great catastrophe, when the earth was still recovering from the gods' wrath, there lived a man named Vukub-Cakix. Arrogant and proud, his name meant "Seven-Times-the-Colour-of-Fire" or "Brilliant One", a reflection of his silver eyes, emerald teeth, and body adorned with precious metals. Believing himself superior to the sun and the moon, he angered the gods with his vanity.

His two sons, Zipacna and Cabrakan, were no less troublesome. Zipacna could raise mountains, while Cabrakan caused earthquakes, further provoking the gods. To put an end to their arrogance, the twin hero-gods, Hun-Ahpu and Xbalanque, descended to earth to humble Vukub-Cakix and his offspring.

Vukub-Cakix sustained himself by eating the round, yellow, fragrant fruit of a tree known as "nanze" or "tapal". One day, upon discovering that Hun-Ahpu and Xbalanque had raided his tree, he confronted them in fury.

As he approached, the hero-gods, hidden in the branches, launched an ambush, wounding him. The blow was so severe that Vukub-Cakix fell from the tree, badly injuring his jaw. Enraged, he fought back, tearing off Hun-Ahpu's arm and torturing him before succumbing to his own injuries.

To recover Hun-Ahpu's arm, the twins sought the help of Xpiyacoc and Xmucane, two wise elders disguised as sorcerers. They tricked Vukub-Cakix into undergoing surgery, replacing his magnificent emerald teeth with ordinary maize kernels. Deprived of his power and vanity, he weakened and eventually died, along with his wife, Chimalmat.

With Vukub-Cakix gone, the hero-gods turned to his sons. Zipacna, who boasted of creating mountains, was lured into a trap set by four hundred young warriors. The twins helped the warriors deceive Zipacna, leading him into a collapsed cave, where he was buried alive.

Meanwhile, Cabrakan, the earthquake god, was tricked into eating poisoned food. Once weakened, he was buried in the earth, ensuring he could no longer wreak havoc.

Thus, the arrogant family of Vukub-Cakix was vanquished, their pride shattered, and balance restored to the world, all thanks to the heroic deeds of Hun-Ahpu and Xbalanque.

Popol Vuh – Book 2

This story (along with the following story) has been adapted from a tale originally told by Thomas A. Janvier in Legends Of The City Of Mexico, published in 1910 by Harper & Brothers Publishers, New York. Legends of the City of Mexico delves into the rich cultural heritage of Mexico, exploring the myths and legends that have been passed down through generations. The book included a diverse range of stories, drawing from Aztec, Spanish, and indigenous Mexican traditions.

The creator deities, Xpiyacoc and Xmucane, were revered as the father and mother of all. They had two sons, Hunhun-Ahpu and Vukub-Hunahpu. Hunhun-Ahpu, who may have been of dual nature, had two sons with his wife Xbakiyalo, Hunbatz and Hunchouen, both known for their wisdom and artistic talents. The family delighted in games of dice and ball, often under the watchful eye of Voc, the messenger of Hurakan.

After Xbakiyalo's death, Hunhun-Ahpu and Vukub-Hunahpu left their sons behind and went to play ball near the underworld, Xibalba.

Their skill and enthusiasm caught the attention of the lords of Xibalba, Hun-Came and Vukub-Came, who, feeling threatened, challenged them to a game with the intention of humiliating them.

Determined to secure their defeat, the Xibalban lords sent four owl messengers to summon the brothers. Despite a tearful farewell to their family, Hunhun-Ahpu and Vukub-Hunahpu followed the owls, descending from Ninxor Carchah into the underworld. Along the way, they crossed a river of blood and were misled by wooden figures at the Xibalban court. Subjected to harsh trials, the brothers were eventually sacrificed and buried.

Hunhun-Ahpu's severed head was hung on a sacred tree, which soon bore fruit forbidden to all in Xibalba, except for one brave soul.

That soul was Xquiq, daughter of Cuchumaquiq, who dared to pluck the forbidden fruit. As she did, Hunhun-Ahpu's head spat into her hand, causing her to conceive. Her miraculous pregnancy enraged the rulers of Xibalba, who ordered her execution. However, through cunning and persuasion, she convinced her executioners to spare her life and managed to escape.

She sought refuge with Xmucane, the mother of Hunhun-Ahpu, who at first refused to believe her story. To prove herself, Xquiq performed a miracle, earning Xmucane's trust. She soon gave birth to twin sons, Hun-Ahpu and Xbalanque. However, their grandmother did not welcome them, as their cries annoyed her, leading to their expulsion from the house.

Growing up in the wild, Hun-Ahpu and Xbalanque developed into skilled hunters and musicians. They soon punished those who had mistreated them, transforming their envious older brothers into apes. Xmucane, filled with sorrow, was told that she could see their faces one last time if she managed to keep from laughing, but she failed, losing her chance forever.

As they matured, the twins were tasked with agricultural work. However, their crops refused to grow, and their efforts met constant setbacks. One day, a rat, which the twins had previously spared, revealed the secret of their family's past, including their father's fate. Armed with new knowledge and tools, the twins set out to reclaim their father's legacy at the sacred ball court.

When Hun-Ahpu and Xbalanque entered Xibalba, the underworld lords grew fearful. They tried to trick the twins into deadly traps, but the brothers used their intelligence and magic to outwit the Xibalbans at every turn. They endured numerous trials, each more difficult than the last, but they never failed. Their resilience infuriated the lords of Xibalba.

Eventually, the twins revealed their true identities and punished the rulers for their past crimes. Having avenged their father, Hun-Ahpu and Xbalanque ascended to the heavens, where they became the sun and the moon. Their defeated enemies were cast into the sky, becoming mere stars.

Back on Earth, Xmucane anxiously watched the canes planted by the twins, as they were tied to their fate. The state of the canes reflected their well-being, bending and withering whenever they faced danger, standing tall when they triumphed.

As Hun-Ahpu and Xbalanque fulfilled their destiny in Xibalba, their grandmother's emotions rose and fell with their struggles.

Thus ends the Second Book of the legend.

Popol Vuh – Book 3

The Creator, known as the Former, shaped four perfect men from yellow and white maize They were Balam-Quitzé (Tiger with the Sweet Smile), Balam-Agab (Tiger of the Night), Mahucutah (The Distinguished Name), and Iqi-Balam (Tiger of the Moon)

These men were not born in the usual way; instead, they were crafted miraculously by the Former's divine hands. However, their perfection and vast knowledge unsettled the Creator. Concerned that they might aspire to godhood, the gods decided to limit their vision, preventing them from seeing the whole world.

While they slept, Hurakan, the god of wind, cast a veil of clouds over their eyes. When they awoke, they found four women had been created to be their wives. These were Caha-Paluma (Falling Water), Choimha (Beautiful Water), Tzununiha (House of the Water), and Cakixa (Water of Aras or Parrots)

From these couples descended the Kichés, the first and most prominent of many peoples.

In the early days, the Kichés lacked knowledge of worship, yet they prayed to the Creator for peace and the return of the sun, which had mysteriously vanished. Their prayers led them on a journey to Tulan-Zuiva, where they received gods assigned to their family groups. Balam-Quitzé received Tohil. Balam-Agab received Avilix. Mahucutah received Hacavitz. However, Iqi-Balam, who had no family, was not given a god.

Life in Tulan was harsh. The Kichés suffered from cold, famine, and the loss of their common language, making communication difficult. Under Tohil's guidance, they set out to find a new home, crossing mountains and a miraculously divided sea.

Eventually, they arrived at Mount Hacavitz, where they witnessed the return of the sun. The sight filled them with joy, marking the birth of the celestial bodies and the beginning of a new era.

As the first men aged, they began to receive visions instructing them to offer human sacrifices. They raided neighbouring villages, seizing captives to offer to their gods. However, they were not alone in battle, for swarms of wasps and hornets, sent by the gods, overwhelmed their enemies, forcing them into submission and tribute.

As their final days approached, the first men gathered their descendants, imparting their wisdom and last words. Together, they sang the Kamucu, the song of "We See," which they had sung when they first beheld the dawn.

After bidding farewell to their wives and children, they vanished, leaving behind a bundled form known as the "Majesty Enveloped."

And thus, the first men of the Kichés passed away, their legacy forever woven into the fabric of their people's history.

Historical Notes

This section contains some brief biographical notes about the original collectors and their books featured in this collection. These notes have been adapted from various digital sources along with other supporting written sources and notes.

Charles F. Lummis

Charles Fletcher Lummis was an American journalist, author, photographer, ethnographer, and preservationist known for his contributions to the preservation of Southwestern American culture and his advocacy for Native American rights.

Charles Fletcher Lummis was born on March 1, 1859, in Lynn, Massachusetts, USA. He was the eldest child of Henry Swift Lummis, a clergyman, and Harriet B. Lummis. Lummis showed a keen interest in literature, history, and culture from an early age, and he pursued his passion for writing throughout his life.

After attending Harvard University for two years, Lummis left without graduating to pursue a career in journalism. In 1884, he began working as a reporter for the *Los Angeles Times* in California.

Lummis quickly gained recognition for his colourful and evocative writing style, which captured the spirit of the American Southwest.

Lummis embarked on a remarkable journey in 1884, walking over 3,500 miles from Cincinnati, Ohio, to Los Angeles, California, in what he called a "tramp across the continent." This adventure, which took him over a year to complete, provided him with firsthand experience of the diverse landscapes, cultures, and peoples of the American West.

Throughout his career, Lummis developed a deep appreciation for the culture, history, and traditions of the American Southwest. He became a passionate advocate for the preservation of Southwestern American culture and heritage, particularly the traditions of Native American communities.

Lummis documented his experiences and observations through writing, photography, and ethnographic research. He founded the Southwest Museum in Los Angeles in 1907, which became a leading institution for the study and preservation of Native American artifacts and art.

In addition to his journalistic and ethnographic work, Lummis was a prolific author and poet. He wrote numerous books, articles, and essays on a wide range of topics, including Southwestern American history, Native American culture, and the Spanish missions of California.

One of Lummis's most famous works is his autobiography, *A Tramp Across the Continent* (1892), which chronicles his epic journey from Cincinnati to Los Angeles. The book became a bestseller and established Lummis as a prominent literary figure.

Charles F. Lummis continued to be actively involved in journalism, cultural preservation, and advocacy throughout his life. He remained dedicated to promoting awareness and appreciation for the cultural heritage of the American Southwest until his death.

Lummis passed away on November 24, 1928, in Los Angeles, California, leaving behind a lasting legacy as a pioneering journalist, author, ethnographer, and cultural preservationist.

Select Bibliography:

- Birch Bark Poems (1883): A collection of Lummis's early poetry.
- A New Mexico David and Other Stories & Sketches of the Southwest (1891): A compilation of stories and sketches reflecting the life and culture of the Southwest. ￼
- Some Strange Corners of Our Country: The Wonderland of the Southwest (1892): Explores the unique landscapes and mysteries of the Southwestern United States.
- A Tramp Across the Continent (1892): Chronicles Lummis's journey on foot from Cincinnati to Los Angeles, offering insights into the diverse regions he traversed.
- The Land of Poco Tiempo (1893): Discusses the culture, environment, and challenges of the Southwestern United States.
- The Spanish Pioneers (1893): Highlights the contributions of Spanish explorers and settlers in America.
- The Man Who Married the Moon and Other Pueblo Indian Folk-Stories (1894): A collection of traditional Pueblo Indian tales. ￼
- My Friend Will (1894): Details are limited, but this work is listed among Lummis's publications.

- The Gold Fish of Gran Chimu: A Novel (1896): A novel set in South America, reflecting Lummis's interest in the region.

- The Enchanted Burro: Stories of New Mexico & South America (1897): A compilation of stories set in New Mexico and South America.

- The Awakening of a Nation: Mexico of To-Day (1898): Provides an analysis of contemporary Mexico during Lummis's time.

- The King of the Broncos and Other Stories of New Mexico (1897): A collection of stories centred on New Mexico.

- Pueblo Indian Folk-Stories (1910): Further explores the folklore of the Pueblo Indians.

- Mesa, Cañon and Pueblo (1925): Describes the landscapes and cultures of the Southwestern United States.

- A Bronco Pegasus: Poems (1928): A collection of Lummis's poetry.

- Flowers of Our Lost Romance (1929): One of his later works, details are limited.

- General Crook and the Apache Wars (1966): Published posthumously, this work discusses General Crook's involvement in the Apache Wars

- Dateline Fort Bowie: Charles Fletcher Lummis Reports on an Apache War (1979): A collection of Lummis's reports on the Apache Wars.

Frona Eunice Wait

Frona Eunice Wait was an American author and educator known for her contributions to literature and her advocacy for women's rights and education.

Frona Eunice Wait was born on October 16, 1859, in Concord, New Hampshire, USA. She was the daughter of John and Eunice Wait, and she grew up in a supportive and intellectually stimulating environment. Wait developed a love for reading and writing at an early age, which set the foundation for her future career as an author and educator.

Wait pursued her education at Wellesley College, where she graduated with honours in 1881. After completing her studies, she began her career as a teacher, initially working in public schools in Massachusetts and New Hampshire.

In 1885, Wait joined the faculty of Wellesley College as an instructor in English literature. She quickly distinguished herself as a dedicated and innovative educator, inspiring her students with her passion for literature and writing. Wait's teaching career spanned over three decades, during which she made significant contributions to the field of education and women's empowerment.

In addition to her work as an educator, Frona Eunice Wait was also an accomplished author and advocate for women's rights. She wrote several books, essays, and articles on topics ranging from literature and education to feminism and social reform. Wait's writing often reflected her commitment to promoting gender equality and empowering women to pursue their intellectual and creative passions.

One of Wait's most notable works is her book *Girls and Education* (1892), in which she examined the importance of education in shaping the lives and opportunities of young women. The book addressed various aspects of women's education, including curriculum development, teaching methods, and the role of education in promoting social and economic equality.

Frona Eunice Wait retired from teaching in 1916 but remained active in literary and educational circles throughout her life. She continued to write and advocate for women's rights, contributing articles and essays to newspapers and journals.

Frona Eunice Wait passed away on December 20, 1942, leaving behind a legacy as a pioneering educator, author, and advocate for women's empowerment.

Select Bibliography:

- Yermah the Dorado: The Story of a Lost Race (1897): A novel intertwining the legend of Atlantis with pre-Columbian America, portraying a highly civilized tribe with spiritual beliefs akin to Christianity.
- The Stories of El Dorado (1904): A collection of tales exploring the myths and legends surrounding the fabled city of gold.
- The Kingship of Mt. Lassen (1922): A historical account detailing the significance of Mt. Lassen, the only active volcano on the U.S. mainland at the time, and its impact on California's development.
- In Old Vintage Days (1937): A reflective work discussing the history and traditions of California's wine industry, complemented by decorations from Dorothy Payne.
- Wines and Vines of California; Or, a Treatise on the Ethics of Wine Drinking (1889): An insightful examination of

California's viticulture and the cultural aspects of wine consumption.

Frank Hamilton Cushing

Frank Hamilton Cushing was an American anthropologist, archaeologist, and ethnologist known for his pioneering work with the Zuni people of New Mexico and his contributions to the study of Native American culture and society.

Frank Hamilton Cushing was born on July 22, 1857, in Northeast Township, Pennsylvania, USA. He grew up in a rural farming community and developed a keen interest in natural history, archaeology, and anthropology from an early age. Despite facing financial hardships, Cushing pursued his passion for learning and self-education, reading extensively on topics related to anthropology and Native American culture.

In 1875, at the age of 18, Cushing began his career in anthropology as a volunteer at the Smithsonian Institution in Washington, D.C. His talent and enthusiasm for the field quickly caught the attention of influential anthropologists, including John Wesley Powell and Lewis Henry Morgan.

In 1879, Cushing joined the United States Geological Survey as a special agent and was assigned to conduct ethnographic research among the Zuni people of New Mexico. He lived among the Zuni for five years, immersing himself in their culture, language, and daily life. Cushing was adopted into the Zuni tribe and given the name "Medicine Flower."

During his time with the Zuni, Cushing made significant contributions to the study of Native American culture and society. He conducted extensive fieldwork, documenting Zuni religious practices, social organization, material culture, and oral traditions. Cushing's work with the Zuni provided valuable insights into the complexity and richness of Indigenous cultures in North America.

In addition to his ethnographic research, Cushing also conducted archaeological excavations at the ancient Pueblo site of Pueblo Bonito in Chaco Canyon, New Mexico. His excavations, carried out in the late 19th century, revealed important insights into the architecture, settlement patterns, and social organization of the ancestral Puebloan people.

Frank Hamilton Cushing's work with the Zuni and his archaeological research at Pueblo Bonito had a lasting impact on the field of anthropology. His detailed ethnographic accounts and archaeological findings contributed to a deeper understanding of Native American cultures and the prehistoric Southwest.

Despite his significant contributions to anthropology, Cushing faced criticism and controversy during his career, particularly regarding his unorthodox methods and controversial theories. However, his pioneering work laid the foundation for future research in anthropology and archaeology.

Frank Hamilton Cushing passed away on April 10, 1900, at the age of 42, leaving behind a legacy as one of the most influential figures in the early development of American anthropology.

Select Bibliography:

- Zuni Folk Tales (1901): A collection of traditional stories from the Zuni people, providing insights into their cultural narratives.
- Outlines of Zuñi Creation Myths (1896): An exploration of the creation beliefs held by the Zuni, detailing their cosmological perspectives.

- My Adventures in Zuñi (1941): A personal account of Cushing's experiences living among the Zuni, offering a unique perspective on their society.
- Zuni Breadstuff (1920): An in-depth study of the agricultural practices and significance of maize in Zuni culture.
- Zuñi Fetiches (1883): An analysis of the symbolic objects used in Zuni rituals, shedding light on their religious practices.
- A Study of Pueblo Pottery as Illustrative of Zuñi Culture Growth (1886): Examines the development of pottery techniques among the Zuni as a reflection of their cultural evolution.
- Exploration of Ancient Key-Dweller Remains on the Gulf Coast of Florida (1896): Documents Cushing's archaeological findings on the Gulf Coast, offering insights into ancient Floridian cultures.
- Zuni Coyote Tales (1998): A compilation of Zuni stories centred around the figure of the coyote, reflecting the tribe's oral traditions.
- The Mythic World of the Zuni (1988): Explores the rich tapestry of Zuni mythology and its role in their cultural identity.
- Short Works of Frank Hamilton Cushing (2004): A collection of Cushing's shorter writings, encompassing various aspects of his anthropological research.

Thomas A. Janvier

Thomas Allibone Janvier was an American writer, journalist, and historian known for his contributions to literature, particularly in the genres of travel writing, fiction, and historical non-fiction.

Thomas Allibone Janvier was born on July 16, 1849, in Philadelphia, Pennsylvania, USA. He grew up in a cultured and literary environment, surrounded by books and encouraged to pursue his interests in writing and literature from an early age. Janvier attended private schools in Philadelphia and later studied at the University of Pennsylvania.

After completing his education, Janvier began his career as a journalist, working for various newspapers and magazines in Philadelphia and New York City. He gained recognition for his vivid and engaging writing style, which combined elements of storytelling with keen observation and descriptive detail.

Janvier's work as a journalist took him to various parts of the United States and Europe, where he wrote about his travels and experiences for popular publications of the time. His travel articles and essays were widely read and appreciated for their literary merit and informative content.

In addition to his journalism, Thomas A. Janvier was also a prolific author of fiction and non-fiction works. He wrote novels, short stories, essays, and historical narratives, drawing inspiration from his travels and experiences as well as his interest in history and culture.

Janvier's fiction often explored themes of adventure, romance, and cultural exchange, with settings ranging from the American Southwest to Europe and Latin America. His best-known works include *In Old New York* (1894), a collection of historical tales set in colonial and early 19th-century New York City, and *The Aztec Treasure-House* (1890), a novel set in Mexico during the Spanish colonial period.

Thomas A. Janvier was also a respected historian and cultural commentator, with a particular focus on the history and culture of New York City and the American Southwest. He wrote extensively about the early history of New York City, exploring topics such as Dutch colonialism, the American Revolution, and the city's growth and development in the 19th century.

Janvier's historical narratives and cultural studies were praised for their meticulous research, engaging narrative style, and insightful analysis. He played a significant role in popularizing the history and culture of New York City and the American Southwest, contributing to a greater understanding and appreciation of these regions.

Thomas Allibone Janvier passed away on June 18, 1913, in New York City, leaving behind a legacy as a versatile and accomplished writer, journalist, and historian.

Select Bibliography:

- Color Studies (1885): A collection of stories depicting artist life, reflecting the vibrant cultural scene of New York's Latin Quarter.
- The Mexican Guide (1886): A comprehensive travel guide to Mexico, offering insights into its culture, history, and landmarks.
- The Aztec Treasure House: A Romance of Contemporaneous Antiquity (1890): A novel intertwining adventure and archaeology, exploring the mysteries of Aztec civilization.

- Stories of Old New Spain (1891): A compilation of tales set in colonial Mexico, highlighting its rich history and culture.
- The Uncle of an Angel, and Other Stories (1891): A collection of short stories showcasing Janvier's narrative versatility and keen observation of human nature.
- An Embassy to Provence (1893): A travelogue detailing the customs, landscapes, and people of Provence, France.
- In Old New York (1894): A historical account of New York City, capturing its evolution and character during the colonial and early national periods.
- In the Sargasso Sea (1898): A novel about a sailor's survival and adventure in the mysterious Sargasso Sea, contributing to the sea fiction genre.
- The Passing of Thomas, and Other Stories (1900): A collection of narratives exploring themes of change and tradition.
- In Great Waters: Four Stories (1901): A compilation of maritime tales reflecting Janvier's fascination with the sea.
- The Christmas Kalends of Provence (1902): A work delving into the festive traditions of Provence, showcasing Janvier's interest in regional cultures.
- The Dutch Founding of New York (1903): An exploration of the Dutch influence on the establishment and development of New York City.
- Santa Fé's Partner: Being Some Memorials of Events in a New-Mexican Track-end Town (1907): A series of linked stories set in New Mexico, reflecting the region's unique cultural landscape.
- Henry Hudson: A Brief Statement of His Aims and His Achievements (1909): A concise biography of the explorer Henry Hudson, examining his contributions to exploration.

- Legends of the City of Mexico (1910): A collection of Mexican legends, offering readers a glimpse into the country's rich folklore.
- From the South of France (1912): Short stories inspired by the culture and scenery of southern France.
- At the Casa Napoleon (1914): A posthumously published work containing a memoir by Ripley Hitchcock, reflecting on Janvier's life and career.

Henry Wysham Lanier

Henry Wysham Lanier was an American author, journalist, and historian known for his contributions to literature, particularly in the genres of travel writing, biography, and historical non-fiction.

Henry Wysham Lanier was born on November 3, 1873, in Baltimore, Maryland, USA. He was the son of Sidney Lanier, a prominent poet and musician, and Mary Day Lanier. Growing up in a literary household, Henry was exposed to a rich cultural environment from a young age, fostering his love for literature and writing.

Lanier attended private schools in Baltimore and later studied at Johns Hopkins University, where he pursued his interests in history, literature, and journalism. He demonstrated a keen intellect and a talent for writing, which would shape his future career as an author and journalist.

After completing his education, Henry W. Lanier began his career as a journalist, working for newspapers and magazines in Baltimore and later in New York City. He wrote articles and essays on a wide range of topics, including literature, travel, history, and current events.

Lanier's work as a journalist took him to various parts of the United States and Europe, where he wrote about his travels and experiences for popular publications of the time. His travel articles and essays were widely read and appreciated for their literary quality and informative content.

In addition to his journalism, Henry Wysham Lanier was also an accomplished author and historian. He wrote several books, biographies, and historical narratives, drawing inspiration from his travels, experiences, and interests.

Lanier's books covered a diverse range of subjects, including biography, history, and travel. He wrote biographies of notable figures such as Edgar Allan Poe and Napoleon Bonaparte, as well as historical narratives exploring various periods and events in American and European history.

Henry W. Lanier's contributions to literature and history were characterized by meticulous research, engaging narrative style, and insightful analysis. He played a significant role in popularizing the history and culture of the United States and Europe, contributing to a greater understanding and appreciation of these regions.

Lanier's books and articles were praised for their vivid descriptions, attention to detail, and ability to bring history to life for readers. His works continue to be studied and enjoyed by readers interested in American and European literature, history, and culture.

Henry Wysham Lanier passed away on May 8, 1937, leaving behind a legacy as a versatile and accomplished writer, journalist, and historian.

Select Bibliography:

- A Book of Giants: Tales of Very Tall Men of Myth, Legend, History, and Science (1922): A collection exploring stories of giants across various cultures and histories.
- The Little Girl Who Dared: A narrative focusing on themes of bravery and adventure.
- A Century of Banking in New York, 1822–1922: An analysis of the evolution of banking practices in New York over a hundred-year period.
- Shakespeare and His Forerunners: Studies in Elizabethan Poetry and Its Development from Early English: A scholarly

examination of Shakespeare's influences and the progression of Elizabethan poetry.

- The Romance of Piscator: A work delving into the art and passion of fishing, reflecting Lanier's appreciation for the sport.
- Greenwich Village: Today & Yesterday (1949): A detailed account of the history and cultural significance of New York's Greenwich Village.

Lewis Spence

Lewis Spence was a Scottish author, journalist, and folklorist known for his prolific writings on mythology, folklore, and the occult. Here's a detailed biography of Lewis Spence:

Lewis Spence was born on November 25, 1874, in Monifieth, Scotland. He grew up in a family with a strong interest in literature and history, which influenced his own passion for storytelling and research. Spence was largely self-educated, devouring books on mythology, folklore, and ancient history from a young age.

In his early career, Lewis Spence worked as a journalist, writing for various newspapers and magazines in Scotland and England. He contributed articles on a wide range of topics, including literature, history, and culture, and gained recognition for his engaging writing style and breadth of knowledge.

Spence's work as a journalist provided him with the opportunity to travel and explore different regions, including Europe and North Africa. His travels sparked his interest in mythology, folklore, and the occult, leading him to delve deeper into these subjects through research and writing.

Lewis Spence's most significant contributions were in the field of mythology and folklore. He wrote extensively on these topics, producing numerous books and articles that explored the myths, legends, and traditions of various cultures around the world.

One of Spence's most famous works is *The Mythology of Ancient Britain and Ireland* (1910), a comprehensive study of the mythological traditions of the British Isles. In this book, Spence examined the origins, themes, and symbolism of British and Irish myths, drawing on archaeological evidence, historical sources, and comparative mythology.

Spence also wrote on a wide range of other mythological and folkloric subjects, including Norse mythology, Celtic folklore, Arthurian legends, and the occult. His works were characterized by their meticulous research, accessible writing style, and enthusiasm for the subject matter.

In his later years, Lewis Spence continued to write and research, producing numerous books and articles on mythology, folklore, and related topics. He also lectured on these subjects and participated in various academic and literary circles.

Spence's contributions to the study of mythology and folklore continue to be valued by scholars, writers, and enthusiasts alike. His books remain popular among readers interested in ancient traditions, cultural history, and the mysteries of the human imagination.

Lewis Spence passed away on March 3, 1955.

Select Bibliography:

- Atlantis and Lost Continents
    - The Problem of Atlantis (1924)
    - Atlantis in America (1925)
    - The History of Atlantis (1927)
    - The Problem of Lemuria: The Sunken Continent of the Pacific (1932)
- Mythology and Folklore
    - The Popol Vuh: The Mythic & Heroic Sagas of the Kichés of Central America (1908)
    - A Dictionary of Mythology (1910)
    - The Myths of Mexico and Peru (1913
    - The Myths of the North American Indians (1914)
    - Myths & Legends of Babylonia & Assyria (1916)

- - Legends & Romances of Brittany (1917)
  - Legends & Romances of Spain (circa 1920)
  - An Introduction to Mythology (1921)
  - The Gods of Mexico (1923)
  - The Mysteries of Egypt: Secret Rites & Traditions of the Nile (1929)
  - The Magic & Mysteries of Mexico (1932)
  - The Minor Traditions of British Mythology (1948)
  - British Fairy Origins: The Genesis & Development of Fairy Legends in British Tradition (1946)
  - Fairy Tradition in Britain (1948)
  - Hero Tales & Legends of the Rhine
  - Ancient Egyptian Myths & Legends (1915)
  - Scottish Ghosts & Goblins (1952)
- **Occultism**
  - An Encyclopaedia of Occultism (1920)
  - Occult Causes of the Present War (1940)
  - Second Sight: Its History & Origins (1951)
- **Ancient Britain**
  - The Mysteries of Britain: Secret Rites & Traditions of Ancient Britain Restored (1905)
  - The Magic Arts in Celtic Britain (1949)
  - Celtic Spells & Charms
  - The History & Origins of Druidism (1949
- **Poetry**
  - The Phoenix (1923)
  - Plumes of Time (1926)
  - Weirds & Vanities (1927)
  - Collected Poems (1953)

About The Editor

Clive Gilson was born in 1962 into a household steeped in sport and rhythm. His father was a senior amateur and lower-league professional footballer, while his mother, equally formidable, was an award-winning ballroom dancer. Their spirited household didn't just hum with ambition, it danced to it.

After earning a degree in History from Leeds University, Clive took an unexpected turn into the then-nascent world of information technology in the late 1980s. Yet, the call of story and stage never left him. Alongside a thriving tech career, he freelanced as a journalist and book reviewer, earning one small by-line in the national press, and also spent over a decade performing in village halls and professional theatres across the south of England.

A true inheritor of his family's sporting zeal, Clive later pivoted into live sports broadcasting. In the 1990s, he became a trusted rugby 'stato' for the BBC, ITV, EuroSport, and TVNZ, bringing insight and analysis to major tournaments including the Heineken Cup, Six Nations, World Sevens, and Rugby World Cups.

As a writer, Clive has made his mark across genres. His debut novel, *Songs of Bliss*, was published in 2017, followed by *A Solitude of Stars* in 2019. Since then, he has released three acclaimed short story collections, *The Mechanic's Curse*, *The Insomniac Booth*, and, in 2025, *Melodies in Black Ink*.

He is also an award-winning poet and the author of a biography detailing the life of a former professional footballer, namely his father. Since 2018, Clive has served as Managing Editor of the Firesides Tales Project, a global storytelling initiative that has published over 30 collections of folktales, fairy tales, myths, and legends from around the world.

Today, Clive continues to write fiction rich in folklore, memory, and quiet transformation, combining his deep love of narrative with a lifelong fascination with the human spirit.

For more about his work, visit clivegilson.com, where stories are always waiting to be found.

ORIGINAL FICTION BY CLIVE GILSON

- *Songs of Bliss*
- *Out of the Walled Garden*
- *The Mechanic's Curse*
- *The Insomniac Booth*
- *A Solitude of Stars*
- *Melodies In Black Ink*

AS EDITOR – *FIRESIDE TALES* – *Western Europe*

- *Tales From the Land of Dragons* – Welsh Folk & Fairy Tales
- *Tales From the Land of The Brave* – Scottish Folk & Fairy Tales
- *Tales From the Land of Saints And Scholars* – Irish Folk & Fairy Tales
- *Tales From the Land of Hope And Glory* – English Folk & Fairy Tales
- *Tales from Gallia* – French Folk & Fairy Tales

AS EDITOR – *FIRESIDE TALES* – *Northern Europe*

- *Tales From Lands of Snow and Ice* – Scandinavian Folk & Fairy Tales
- *Tales From the Viking Isles* – Icelandic Folk & Fairy Tales
- *Tales From the Forest Lands* – Finnish Folk & Fairy Tales
- *Tales From the Old Norse* – Scandinavian Folk & Fairy Tales
- *Tales from Germania* – German Folk & Fairy Tales

AS EDITOR – *FIRESIDE TALES* – *Southern Europe*

- *Tales From the Land of Rabbits* – Spanish & Portuguese Folk & Fairy Tales
- *Tales Told by Bulls and Wolves* – Italian Folk & Fairy Tales
- *Tales of Fire and Bronze* – Greek Folk & Fairy Tales

AS EDITOR – *FIRESIDE TALES* – *Eastern Europe*

- *Tales From The Samodivi* – Balkan Folk & Fairy Tales
- *Tales From the Land of the Strigoi* – Romanian Folk & Fairy Tales
- *Tales Told by the Wind Mother* – Hungarian Folk & Fairy Tales

AS EDITOR – *FIRESIDE TALES – North America*

- *Okaraxta* - Tales from The Great Plains
- *Tibik-Kìzis* – Tales from The Great Lakes & Canada
- *Jóhonaa'éí* –Tales from America's Southwest
- *Qugaaĝix̂* - First Nation Tales from Alaska & The Arctic
- *Karahkwa* - First Nation Tales from America's Eastern States
- *Pot-Likker* - Folklore, Fairy Tales, and Settler Stories from America

AS EDITOR – *FIRESIDE TALES – Africa*

- *Arokin Tales* – Folklore & Fairy Tales from West Africa
- *Hadithi Tales* – Folklore & Fairy Tales from East Africa
- *Inkathaso Tales* – Folklore & Fairy Tales from Southern Africa
- *Tarubadur Tales* – Folklore & Fairy Tales from North Africa
- *Elephant And Frog* – Folklore from Central Africa

AS EDITOR – *FIRESIDE TALES – Middle East*

- *Tales From The Meddahs* – Turkish Folk & Fairy Tales
- *Tales From The Hakawati* – Arabic Folk & Fairy Tales
- *Tales Told By Balebos & Gusan* – Jewish & Armenian Folk & Fairy Tales

AS EDITOR – *FIRESIDE TALES – Asia & The Far East*

- *Tales Told By The Kathaakaar* – Folk & Fairy Tales from India
- *Tales Of The Gùshì Yuan* – Chinese Folk & Fairy Tales

AS EDITOR – *FIRESIDE TALES – Animal Tales*

- *Dog Tails* – Folk & Fairy Tales featuring our canine chums
- *Cat Tails* – Folk & Fairy Tales featuring our feline friends

AS EDITOR – *FIRESIDE TALES – South & Central America*

- *Tales From The Caribbean* – Folk & Fairy Tales from Caribbean islands
- *Tales From Central America* – Central American Folk & Fairy Tales
- *Tales Told From South America* – South American Folk & Fairy Tales

www.ingramcontent.com/pod-product-compliance
Lightning Source LLC
Chambersburg PA
CBHW060539190726
48283CB00003B/795